Wilderness Wanderer

JENIFER JENNINGS

Editor: Jill Monday

Scripture quotations and paraphrases are taken from the Holy Bible, King James Version, Copyright © 1977, 1984, 2001 by Thomas Nelson, Inc.

This book is a work of historical fiction based closely on real people and events recorded in the Holy Bible. Details that cannot be historically verified are purely products of the author's imagination. Any resemblance to actual persons, living or dead, or actual events is purely coincidental.

ISBN: 978-1-954105-04-1

To those who wander:
May you find the path God has for you.

Chapter 1

"And the people murmured against Moses, saying, 'What shall we drink?' "
-EXODUS 15:24

1446 B.C., Marah

"Moses!" a man's voice blurted from outside the tent. "Come quickly."

Miriam looked at her brother, who stood and rushed out.

"What do you think has happened?" Puah

asked her from her spot across the tent where she had been meeting with Moses.

"I don't know, but we should go see."

The two women hastened after the men.

The man led Moses out of the camp and to a nearby stream where a large group gathered.

"We came to draw water." He pointed to the simple stream. "But the waters are bitter."

Miriam hadn't realized how thirsty she was until she saw the waiting liquid. She walked to the water's edge and bent down.

The stream flowed quietly and looked inviting. The waters reflected back her well-worn face. Her cheeks where flush from the trek and her dark hair stuck out from under her blue headcloth. She reached up to tuck the strands back into place.

With a glance toward her brother, she dipped a cupped hand into the river disturbing the image and lifted the drink to her mouth.

The cool water satisfied her parched tongue, but the bitterness almost made her spit it out. She forced herself to swallow and then wiped her lips on the back of her sleeve.

"I guess we've discovered why they call this place Marah," she whispered to Puah who had joined her.

"What are we going to drink?" a woman in the crowd called behind them.

"We have almost run out of our supply," a man

echoed her concern.

"We can't journey any further without water," another added.

Moses lifted his hands to silence their pleas. "We will ask the Lord for help." He turned to look out over the water and prayed, "Hear our cry, Lord. Provide for Your people as You have promised."

The congregation held their breath.

Miriam watched her brother. His attention raised up as if someone had called his name. She felt the familiar sense she had so many times. God was making His presence known.

"Help me," Moses shouted as he moved over to a tree growing beside the stream. "We need to push this into the waters."

Men and women exchanged glances.

Moses leaned on the slim tree with all his weight.

A few men stepped over to help. Some dug up the roots while others collected on one side to shove. With only a few short movements, they were able to push the tree into the water.

"Try it now," Moses instructed.

Miriam dipped her hand in again. She hesitated as she brought the water to her lips. Her throat tightened at the anticipation of bitterness. She parted her lips and let the cool water flow into her waiting mouth.

The same water she had wanted to spit out was transformed from bitter to sweet. She cupped both hands and lifted as much as she could to drink.

"It's good," she said after a long draw.

"Come," Moses called to the waiting crowd. "Fill your bottles and water pots."

Each took their turn filling up all they could carry.

Moses stood over them. "God has said, 'If you will diligently heed My voice and will do what is right in My sight, giving ear to My commands, and keeping My laws, then I will put none of the diseases upon you which I brought upon the Egyptians. I am Jehovah-Rapha, the God who heals you.' "

After seeing that everyone in camp had enough water, Miriam walked with Puah toward the old midwife's tent. She kept her pace easy allowing the older woman to take her time.

"I heard you delivered the first baby born in freedom today," she inquired.

"Yes." Puah turned slightly toward her. "I suppose I did."

Miriam watched the smile reach all the way to the woman's eyes.

"And my last."

She hesitated with her next step. "Last?"

"Oh my, yes." The midwife wobbled a little as they neared her small tent.

She offered her elbow to steady the older woman.

"My old bones just don't have the strength to keep up with these Hebrew babies," Puah joked as she accepted the extra support.

Miriam chuckled. "I've seen you run circles around your apprentices when a baby is on the way."

She nodded. "In my youth, perhaps." She drew in a long breath and let it out just as slowly. "I officially handed everything over to Eliora before I came to see your brother earlier."

Miriam bit her lip.

"Speak your mind, child," the older woman encouraged. "You never were one for hiding your thoughts."

"I don't hold any ill will toward Eliora. It's just that she's so…" Miriam struggled to convey her concerns.

"Young," Puah finished for her. She waved toward the flap of her tent allowing Miriam to enter first.

"Exactly." She ducked her head slightly to step into the goat-hair tent just big enough for one person.

Puah followed. She hung up the freshly filled skin on the peg of the center tent pole. Then she slowly eased herself down on a small pile of elaborate pillows.

Miriam observed the stack. They were not in her friend's simple taste. Beadwork covered the fine linens chasing itself into a pattern. Tassels hung from the corners of the fabric. No doubt they were part of the haul extracted from the Egyptians the night they left Egypt.

A shiver ran up her spine as she remembered the stories they shared the first few nights in the desert. Puah and her apprentice went from house to house asking the women of Egypt to give up their possessions after the last plague struck. The same women who only hours earlier had discovered their sons dead in their beds. Miriam had not envied the task. She was grateful when Moses and Aaron had her making other preparations which kept her from being part of those who spoiled Egypt of her treasures.

"We were both young once too," Puah spoke on.

"But neither of us were handed an entire guild at her age."

"I understand your concern." Puah adjusted her body and frowned with discomfort. "Our people are heading to the land promised to our father, Abraham. We are promised an abundance of blessings which will also include our numbers."

"And so, we need someone strong to lead the midwives. Who do you think will be there to help deliver most of those babies?"

"I have faith in Eliora. I see so much of myself in her." She stretched up to reach for the pouch that hung above her.

Miriam stood to retrieve the bag. She handed it down to her. "You were trained by the best."

"Are you trying to say that I am not as good as my predecessor?" She received the pouch.

Miriam shook her head. "That's not what I'm saying at all. I just meant that-"

"I know." Puah held up her free hand. "I was fortunate enough to have many more years under Shiphrah than Eliora has had with me." She took a long drink from the wineskin bottle. "Sweetest water I've ever tasted."

Miriam's mouth watered.

Puah offered her the pouch.

She waved it off. "Is there anyone else you'd consider putting in charge instead?"

"It's already done."

"She's only twenty-six!" Miriam lapped the four corners of the tent.

"I know full well how old she is."

She crossed her arms over her chest.

Puah chuckled.

Miriam squinted at her. "It feels as if you're not taking this seriously at all. The fate of our people will be in her hands."

The midwife patted the ground beside her.

Miriam huffed, but obeyed.

"I wasn't laughing at the situation," she explained. "I was laughing at you. You look so much like the small child I first met many years ago. Those gorgeous sparkling eyes of yours peeking out from all that dark hair."

Miriam pushed her hair away from her face.

"There are others I could have given leadership of the guild to, but I didn't."

She opened her mouth, but Puah put her hand up again. "I've prayed about this for a long time. Eliora is the right choice." She reached over and gave Miriam's hand a firm squeeze. "She will guide the women and train them as I have trained her."

"But-"

"And our people's fate will be in God's hands, not hers," Puah interjected.

She sighed. "I suppose you're right."

"I know I am."

"Puah?" a young voice called from the other side of the entrance.

"Come in, Eliora," Puah answered.

The woman dipped her head in. "I'm sorry. I didn't mean to interrupt."

"You're not, young one." She waved to an empty place beside herself. "Miriam and I were just chatting."

"Greetings," Eliora bowed toward Miriam before she knelt beside Puah.

She nodded back. The bright light in the woman's smile and easy movements made her seem all the more childlike to Miriam.

"I brought you some food." Eliora lifted the strap of her bag over her head and extended it toward Puah.

"That was very thoughtful." She accepted the offer. "How's Batya and the baby?"

"Both doing well."

"Good to hear." Puah grazed on pieces of dried fruit and flatbread she retrieved from the bag.

"And how are you?" Eliora observed her mentor.

"Tired, but otherwise well."

"In that case, I won't stay long." She rose and returned the strap over her head to set the bag across her body. "I just wanted to check on you and bring you some food since we had that delivery earlier."

"Thank you."

"I'll head out as well." Miriam stood.

Puah gently grasped her wrist. "Would you stay just a moment longer?"

"Of course."

"Sleep well," Eliora called over her shoulder as she exited the tent.

Puah watched her form disappear.

"What is it?" Miriam asked.

She pulled her back down and leaned into her ear. "Guide her," Puah begged, her voice barely a whisper. "Protect her from harm."

Miriam searched her friend's ancient eyes. "Of course."

"Thank you." Puah relaxed her grip and leaned back on the stack of pillows.

She tilted her head to one side watching the older woman breathe easy. Puah's face showed nothing but contentment and peace.

Miriam was happy to see her friend at ease, but something inside stirred. She didn't feel right, but she couldn't put her finger on exactly what bothered her. Puah had made her decision about the guild leadership and there would be no changing her mind.

Puah opened her eyes and smiled a wide grin.

Miriam could not push the uneasy feeling away long enough to return a smile.

Chapter 2

"And Miriam the prophetess, the sister of Aaron, took a timbrel in her hand; and all the women went out after her with timbrels and with dances."
-EXODUS 15:20

Miriam tossed on her straw mat as a dream filled her unconscious mind.

Fire from their first encampment on the freedom side of the Red Sea lit her vision. She saw Puah and the other women dance around her. She reached out for her friend, but Puah twirled away. She chased her around the fire as both danced more wildly then Miriam had remembered. Puah's laugh filled the cool air.

A deafening scream caused Miriam to sit straight up. She clung to her woven blanket. In the quiet stillness, she couldn't tell if the sound that roused her had come from her dream or reality. It wasn't until another scream pierced her hearing that she knew for sure. Someone was screaming her name.

She stood and flew out of the tent. As soon as she was outside in the first rays of sun coming across the sands, she found the source.

Eliora had her knees dug into the sand right outside the tent. Her face was streaked with a mix of sand and tears. Her mouth was hung open as if she were going to scream again.

"What is it?" Miriam hit her knees beside the younger woman.

"It's…she's…" Eliora's sobs interrupted her explanation.

"Take a deep breath," Miriam instructed.

She obeyed.

"Now, what has you so upset?"

"Puah…" Eliora looked up at her with red, pleading eyes.

The pieces connected all too quickly for Miriam. There was only one thing that would have brought Eliora to the point of such sorrow. Puah was no longer walking this wilderness with them.

"Take me to her," Miriam whispered. Her own tears begged at the corners of her eyes, but she pushed them back.

The two women stood outside the midwife's small tent within a matter of moments.

Miriam watched the flap sway in and out with the wind. She held her breath and ordered her feet to move forward, but she stood still.

Eliora's sobs continued beside her.

Miriam looked to Eliora who kept her eyes on the opening. A hasty and silent plea for strength gave Miriam the will to enter.

Puah's body lay still on her pile of pillows. The same look of peace was still set on her pale face that Miriam had left her with the night before.

The familiar uneasy feeling crept up in her again. It had been a warning, a way to prepare her for what was coming.

Eliora stepped beside her. "I came to see her this morning. We were going together to meet with the guild." She turned toward Miriam. "What am I supposed to tell them?"

"The truth," she offered. "Puah put you in charge for a reason. She trusted your judgment."

Fresh tears streamed down Eliora's face.

"Go to them now." She patted her pointy shoulder. "They will need you."

"I can't leave her." She shook her head.

"I'll see to her until you return."

Eliora turned to leave, but took another glance over her shoulder. "I'll be quick. Please don't start without me."

She nodded.

When Eliora left, Miriam sat at the opening of the tent looking out on the start of the day. People moved about to survive another day in the desert. The sun's rays stretched over them warming their bodies and urging them on.

Miriam pulled her knees up to her chest and rested her chin on them. She closed her eyes at the burning tears. She prayed Eliora would be as quick as she promised. Her heart ached. Her stomach turned and twisted.

She didn't track the sun's movement, but Eliora returned with two other women in what seemed only a few moments.

Miriam recognized the two as leaders in the guild whom Puah had introduced to her before. She always treasured the fact that Puah made it a point to keep both Hebrew and Egyptian women united in her guild. Even when Pharaoh's separation drove them apart, Puah had kept them joined. The two who stood with Eliora represented that bond. One Hebrew and one Egyptian standing together in the face of those trying to divide them.

Though many Egyptian midwives remained in Egypt, several took the offer to trade Egypt for Canaan. Even though they were already free, they felt led to follow a God they barely knew. They had shared as much with her on the journey. Miriam walked with the guild listening as they shared birth stories and hopes for the future.

"Jola. Anzety." She nodded toward the women.

"We've come to help prepare..." Jola started

before she choked back the words.

"We've come to help." Anzety wrapped an arm around Jola' shaky shoulders.

The women worked in silence cleaning and wrapping the body for burial. Each hand moved with skill and grace.

Miriam marveled at the way they worked together without instruction. She hoped the bond would set an example for the rest of the camp. If all of them could work together this well, they might survive the trek toward Canaan.

When the sun had reached its highest point, the women lifted the wrapped body onto a travel cot and set out for the outskirts of camp.

Many eyes watched as they walked through the makeshift streets between groups of tents. Some stopped until they passed while others simply went about their work.

Miriam saw two men standing together by a freshly dug hole when they finally made it to the end of the endless rows of tents.

"Moses sent us," one explained. "He sends word of shared sorrow."

Miriam's heart warmed. Word had reached her brother, their leader, and he had sent the two men ahead to prepare the grave relieving the women from the hard labor.

"It's all ready." The other waved to the sand.

The two men took a step back to make room

for them.

Miriam motioned for the women to set their load down. Then she dared a peek out of the corner of her eye at the carefully wrapped body that lay upon the cot. It was too much for her and she had to look away.

Tears blurred her vision causing the colors of the afternoon to turn into a muddle of orange and browns. She could mourn. There was no law against such a thing. In fact, it was encouraged.

Loud wails of the women around her seemed to echo through the desert. The guild had been informed and they had all come to mourn their shared loss.

She wiped away the warm dampness with the edge of her headwrap. Guilt warred within her. She wanted to mourn the loss too. The woman lying under the burial cloth was a dear friend. One of the bravest and most knowledgeable women she had ever met. She was as fierce as any Hebrew woman and twice as courageous.

Puah.

The mere thought of the name brought tears back to the surface. This time she let them go without pushing them away. Her lips trembled like shaking gates holding back a flood of sorrow.

The midwife had held almost every newborn Hebrew in her calloused, strong hands. She was one of the women Miriam most admired.

She fought to hold her resolve. She was God's prophetess. She was the sister of their leader. She was a leader. If she were going to be taken as seriously as her two younger brothers, then she should be strong enough to show restraint.

Blinking away the tears, her eyes adjusted to the red face of Eliora. Puah had left the entire midwife guild in the young, but capable hands of her apprentice. Puah had whispered a plea into Miriam's ear the last night of her life.

"Guide her," Puah's voice had barely been a whisper. "Protect her from harm."

As if Miriam could protect anyone from their destiny. As if she could stand between anyone and the Creator.

"Of course," Miriam had lied. Oh, she would try, but could she really do anything to stop what lay ahead of every person who walked the earth?

Eliora looked as if she were going to faint. Her bloodshot eyes were fixated on the body. Her dress shook from the trembling figure it covered. Her shoulders were hunched and bobbing up and down in rhythm with her cries.

Miriam looked back at the body. The sight of the clean linen against the sand broke her. She rushed forward tripping over her own sandals and the loose sand. She fell onto the body and let everything that had been held back all day come forth. Her lips parted and a howl unlike any she had ever made was released.

She buried her face in the cloth and cried until she had no more tears left to give. The crowd which encircled her resonated her response with another round of cries and wails.

When the noise settled down, she lifted her head.

The men stood waiting and the women stood watching her.

She rose and brushed the sand from her dress. She nodded once without making eye contact with anyone.

She, along with Eliora, Jola, and Anzety, lifted the body from the cot and placed her into the shallow grave. Kneeling in the warm sand, each pushed handfuls into the hole until the body was completely covered.

Miriam watched as the white cloth disappeared under the sand. It was like watching a backward birth. Then she was gone completely.

After only a few moments of silence, the gathering headed back to the safety of their tent city. Even in their number, they would not be safe outside the camp for long. When the sun set, wild animals would search for a feast. The temperature would drop on some nights to freeze a person to death in a matter of hours.

Miriam stood gazing at the slightly raised mound listening to the footsteps fade behind her.

She assumed she was alone until she heard a sniffle.

She turned to see Eliora staring at the mound as well. Miriam looked back one last time and then stepped to her side. She wrapped an arm around the younger woman and whispered, "There is nothing more we can do here. Let's get back to camp before sunset."

Eliora nodded once and then shifted her weight to lean against Miriam.

They turned away and shuffled back to camp together.

After returning Eliora to her tent, Miriam made her way to her own.

She pushed aside the flap and stepped inside. The front area was empty. She stepped to the goat hair cloth that separated the rooms. It too was vacant. Moses and Aaron were always somewhere else. Elisheba was no doubt in the tent of one of her four sons. Each had married and started families of their own. Her sister-in-law was probably helping with her grandchildren.

She sunk to the ground and wept again. In the privacy of the empty tent, she could openly mourn. Her heart ached for the comfort of her friend. Whenever Miriam felt a burden too heavy to carry, she would find an excuse to visit Puah's tent. Of course, the wise woman always saw through her deception.

Miriam smiled as she could almost see Puah's sideways glance and slight grin edging her lips upward as she played along.

The pain of loss struck through her midsection like fire. She couldn't remember the last time she had eaten. She knew she hadn't taken anything since she had been awakened by Eliora.

The older midwife had sent them both away last night after a visit. She was weak of body, but not of mind.

"How am I to get any rest with you two lingering over me like new mothers? Away with you both," she had ordered upon finding out Eliora waited outside the tent for Miriam.

Puah had brushed them both off with a wave of her hand like Egyptian royalty dismissing someone with whom they had lost interest.

Miriam smiled again. *Concerned for others over herself even to the very end.*

Sobs racked her body. She held herself as if she'd fall to pieces if she didn't hold tight enough. She rocked back and forth, trying to ease the pain she feared would never cease.

"How could you leave me, Puah?" she cried. "I need you."

She laid down on the carpet and closed her eyes.

The dream from the previous night began the same. Fire from their first encampment on the freedom side of the Red Sea lit her imagination. Puah and the other women twirled around her. She tried again to reach out for her friend, but Puah danced away. The chase around the fire continued just as before while Puah's laugh filled the air.

Miriam reached for Puah's flowing dress, but every time the woman danced just out of reach. Her friendly chuckle transformed into a piercing cackle until Miriam had to cover her ears.

She woke up with fresh tears on her cheeks.

The darkness hung heavy around her. It had been some hours, but she had no way of knowing how many.

She moved to a seated position. The pain snarled at her from the edges, lying in wait to pull her under again. Her stomach rumbled from its emptiness. She moved her hands to cover the sound.

"Miriam," a soft voice called from the other side of the curtain.

The sound was vaguely familiar. She tried to clear her parched throat. "Coming," her voice cracked with dryness.

She stood slowly and moved to the front side of the tent.

A woman stood at the entrance with a covered tray in her hands.

"I came to see to you earlier, but your brother

said you were asleep."

A pang of guilt rushed through Miriam. *Did this woman need ministering?*

She shifted on her bare feet.

"Please come in," Miriam waved.

"Thank you." The woman stepped in and placed the tray down at Miriam's feet. "I heard about your midwife friend."

Sorrow edged closer to Miriam's center, but she fought it back.

"I wanted to bring you this." She bent down and uncovered the offering.

Miriam's eyes grazed over the bowls of food and piles of fresh flatbread.

"I remembered your kindness when my father died."

Bilhah.

They had only been free for a few days when the girl's father had died from a sickness. Miriam had gone to the family with food and comfort. It had been one of her first acts as self-appointed leader over the women. Though her brothers encouraged the initiative and praised her tender heart for the people.

"I'm grateful for the gift."

Bilhah smiled brightly for a moment before it faded into a mask of sorrow. "I'll leave you to eat."

Miriam nodded and watched her leave. She sat on her knees next to the tray. The warm scent of freshly baked flatbread filled her nose. It reached out to her like a warm embrace. Her stomach begged in volume again.

"Thank You for Your provision, Lord," she prayed aloud. "Bless Bilhah's hands for her simple offering."

She ripped off a large piece of bread and dug into the waiting meal.

Chapter 3

"And they came to Elim, where were twelve wells of water, and threescore and ten palm trees: and they encamped there by the waters."
-EXODUS 15:27

Miriam's feet slugged through the thick sand. The pack between her shoulders felt heavier than normal. She knew it wasn't the contents of her load, but the emptiness in her soul that weighed her down.

She walked with the midwife guild next to Eliora who had taken their lost leader's place. This was a different march though. They walked in silence out of respect. No one wanted to share stories for fear of sorrow filling the places where Puah's memory would rise to the surface.

The people around them stopped and the sudden halt caught Miriam's attention. She glanced up to find her brother's face. Moses motioned for the people to set up camp where they had stopped.

She stepped closer to him. "Where are we?"

"Elim," he answered, unloading his pack from off his back. "There are plenty of wells here and some palm trees for shade. It's a good place to rest."

She nodded and let her bag down. She stretched her tight back and looked around. The group of people spread out behind her as far as her eyes could see and then some. She was thankful that the people had allowed her to march in peace. Though it had been a few weeks since they left Marah, the pain of her loss was still fresh.

"Miriam," Aaron called.

She made her way over. "Yes, brother."

"Why don't you help Elisheba and the others?" His eyes shone with pity.

"Of course." She turned away from his worried gaze.

When their tent was erected, Miriam went immediately inside. She tucked behind the second curtain to the women's quarters and set up her few items in one corner.

"Miriam," Moses called.

She cringed. She had done all the work she could think of without a complaint. What more could he ask of her today?

She peeled the heavy curtain back and stepped into the front opening. "Yes, brother." She kept her eyes on the rugs that covered the main area.

"Sit," her brother's gruff voice offered.

She obeyed, but kept her eyes to the intricate patterns some Egyptian had woven into the fabric.

"Miriam," Moses started. "I know you are grieving the loss of your friend."

His words stirred the emptiness inside her.

"But our people need you."

She ordered back her tears.

He sighed. "Sister, the time to grieve is over."

She looked up at him. His look was stern, but his eyes were soft, almost pleading. Aaron's face matched his.

"The others…" Moses faltered a bit. "The midwives have finished their grieving and so should you."

"If that is your command."

"I'm not your king, sister." He sighed. "It's my request."

Her eyes found the rugs again.

"I know Puah was a close friend."

The name drove spikes in her heart. The tent shifted around her.

"I know how much she meant to you, but we need you. Our people need you."

"It's true, sister," Aaron agreed. "We all need each other out here in the wilderness."

"What is it you need of me?" She struggled to keep the emotions from escaping that fought their way to the surface.

Moses cleared his throat. "We need a strong example for the women. They trust you, Miriam. They adore you and look to you for guidance. Your sorrow has affected them."

Her attention snapped up to him. She had been so consumed with sadness that she never thought anyone else would suffer because of her sorrow. "How?"

"They see your sadness. They notice your distance and slow pace," Aaron explained.

"Oh," she conceded. "I never realized."

"Be there for them," Aaron offered.

"How?"

Moses rubbed his beard. "Perhaps you can help those most in need."

She tilted her head.

"Those on the outskirts.," he explained. "Many of them are women who don't have family to take care of them. Widows. Those too sick to care for themselves. You could offer them aid."

She thought about some of those she knew who struggled to keep up on the marches. She nodded.

"Then it's settled."

Miriam rose and bowed before returning to her side of the curtain.

It wasn't long before they were moving on from the small oasis they had found. Within a matter of days, the group of Hebrews crossed into the Wilderness of Zin.

Miriam walked among the people as they stopped for a rest. She checked on the widows and made sure they had water and a place to rest. The easy chats and busy work for her hands helped ease her loneliness and sorrow.

"I'm not saying he's a bad person," a man's voice caught her attention as she walked along the path. "I'm simply asking where he is really leading us?"

"Hmm…" another man's deep timbre voice agreed.

"Moses and that brother of his get to call all the shots."

She stepped into the sunlight and followed the sound of the voices.

"I say it's about time we get a say in how things go," the first continued.

"What are you going to do about it?"

"I say we go get our questions answered."

By the time she found the source of the discussion, two men were leaving a tent and heading toward the front of the group.

She followed their hurried pace until they came upon Moses and Aaron.

"What good has come out of us being led into the wilderness?" the first man's voice carried. "It would have been better for us to die by the hand of the Lord in Egypt. At least there we sat by bowls full of meat and filled our stomachs with bread. Out here we are doing nothing but walking and starving."

A crowd formed around them as the man hurled allegations at Moses.

"We've come to the end of what we brought with us out of Egypt. All we have left are our herds, which will not sustain this great multitude for long."

Miriam searched her brother's calm face.

He didn't flinch. He stood and took every hit the man threw with his words.

The men ran out of arrows of accusation and stood waiting for Moses to respond.

"I will inquire of the Lord," Moses said and tucked into the tent behind him.

Miriam stepped closer and reached for the whipping flap. She hesitated. It was her tent too, but would she interrupt if her brother was listening for the voice of God? Would God not speak in her presence?

She peeled back the goatskin and glanced inside.

Moses was on his face in prayer. His words barely above a whisper, but flowed freely. She caught only pieces of the one-sided conversation.

"People...land...bread...flesh...wilderness... please help..." Then he was silent.

His body was so perfectly still anyone else might have guessed he had fallen asleep. Miriam knew better. He was listening to the voice of God.

Her body tingled in response to the voice that she knew he was hearing. A voice she had heard for herself though it took a different form than what her brother heard. He could hear the voice as if it were a friend speaking. She could feel the voice, like the wind that blew her hair or moved the sands. It was a strong, yet gentle stirring that began inside and filled her so completely.

Her brother's form shifted to a seated position and then he rose to his feet.

She released the flap and took a step back.

Moses came out of the tent and walked past his two accusers. He found a place to stand so many could hear him.

Miriam stood nearby.

"I have heard from the Lord," Moses said in his commanding voice. "Behold, He will rain bread from heaven for us. Everyone will go out and gather a specific rate every day. This will be a test of obedience. Every day for five days, you will collect the same rate.

"On the sixth day, you will gather and prepare twice as much because there will not be any provided on the seventh day. The Lord will give you flesh to eat in the evening and in the morning bread to the full. In the morning, you will see the glory of the Lord, the One who brought you out of Egypt."

He looked down at the two men. "Your murmurings are not against us, but against the Lord." Then he looked to his brother. "Call all the congregation to come near."

Aaron spread word quickly for the people to gather.

Moses pointed toward the wilderness where the cloud of glory appeared. "The Lord has heard your murmurings and will give you flesh to eat this evening."

The cloud moved and kicked up the wind. Then the sound of flapping wings filled the air.

Miriam covered her face against the wind, but peered between her fingers to watch the cloud.

The wind pushed quail close to them. Birds covered the ground.

She reached out and caught one by the neck. Other quail surrounded her. They stood perfectly still as if willing to die.

The two men who had stirred the people grabbed as many birds as they could and ran toward their tents.

Miriam shook the bird in her hand. It barely fluttered. It was like a young lamb. Completely submissive and ignorant of its fate.

She studied the round muscles of the bird. His feathers clean and bright shone in the rays of the sun.

She wasn't a good hunter. Never had to be one in the land of Egypt. She could have spent months hunting in the desert and never have come up with a prize such as he. He cooed softly in her grasp. She brushed his ruffled feathers down. He was brown and beautiful. Plump and ready for feasting.

She hurried to her tent, her mouth filling with saliva at the anticipation of meat. There wasn't much she envied about Egyptians, but their rich diet was certainly something anyone would admire.

She reached the tent in time to see Moses and Aaron entering with handfuls of birds as well. She went in and showed off her prize. The men handed off their catches to Elisheba.

She walked over to her sister-in-law. "I'll take them outside," she offered.

Elisheba's wrinkled face lit up. "Thank you. It's been a while since I dressed a bird."

Miriam looked to the group. "Do you think we need all of them?"

"Aaron has invited the boys to join us."

"Then I hope we have enough."

"I might go grab another one." Elisheba

chuckled.

Miriam took the birds out of the tent. She feared they might flee if she released them, but they didn't. They simply sat down as soon as she set them in the sand.

For a moment, she wondered if something was wrong with the birds. A typical bird would have stayed far away from a large gathering of people. Yet the birds flew straight into camp and covered the ground around their feet. Even now they stayed still as if held in place by an unseen force.

"I know this has to be You, Lord," she prayed. "There is no other explanation."

She reached for her male. He willingly yielded under her hand. He didn't limp, he didn't fight. She felt a pang of sadness that such a creature had to die.

For you. The familiar presence whispered inside.

She took a deep breath and broke its neck. The bird didn't make a sound. Neither did the others when their turn came. She collected the group and brought them around to the side where Elisheba was stoking a new fire.

Miriam set them down beside a large bowl and got to work plucking. Before long, she had cleaned each bird entirely and had a fine collection of feathers.

Elisheba looked at the pile. "That'd make a

nice pillow."

Miriam wiped her greasy hand on a piece of cloth and then inspected the feathers. She lifted a brown one and examined it. She was sure it had come from her prize male. Its clean lines and shiny gloss were a testimony to its health. "Yes," she agreed. "They sure would."

Elisheba cleaned and skewered the birds on a rod. Then she set them over the fire and turned them.

Miriam watched as the skin slowly faded from pale to golden. It was like watching a beautiful sunrise. The fire spat and snapped as the grease from the birds dripped into it.

Elisheba kept a steady rotation to ensure even cooking on each bird.

The scent of crisping flesh sent Miriam's mouth watering again and her stomach into flips. She hadn't realized how hungry she was. She had eaten little since they left Marah. Every time she took a bowl, she remembered her last night with Puah and her appetite waned. The smells and sights of cooking flesh brought back her appetite with a vengeance as if it had been angry with her for being sent away so long.

"Almost there," Elisheba said as she checked the meat.

Miriam's appetite chomped at her. If she were alone, she might have ripped the rod from the fire and set to work eating the scorching flesh right then and there. She wasn't sure if it were manners or God keeping her steady, but she was grateful for either.

"There we are," Elisheba said. She reached for the large platter in Miriam's hand.

Miriam looked down. She hadn't realized she was digging her fingernails into the wood. She held it out and accepted the birds as her sister-in-law slid each off in turn.

The weight lowered Miriam's arm. Warmth radiated against her chest. The delicious aroma filled her nose. She longed to bite into the flesh that waited for her. Her prize male's breast lay in the center faced up at her.

She heard Elisheba clear her throat.

Miriam's attention dragged away from the meat. She followed her into the tent and set the tray before her brothers and their guests.

After a few moments of thanksgiving led by Moses, the group feasted on the provided flesh.

Miriam reached over and pulled off a hunk of her bird's breast. The warmth tingled her fingers. She bit into the meat. Heat radiated through her mouth, down her throat, and into her waiting stomach. It was the most satisfying moment she could recall. Bite after bite was more satisfying. She didn't slow down. She didn't enter into the conversation that flowed around her. She only ate mouthful after mouthful of flesh. She refused the bread and other meager portions they had scrounged for to accompany their meal. She only indulged in the flesh of her prized catch until she found herself licking his bones to remove every remaining drop of deliciousness.

Chapter 4

*"Then said the LORD unto Moses, 'Behold, I
will rain bread from heaven for you;' "*
-EXODUS 16:4

Miriam rolled onto her back. The night had been
filled with dreamless, restful sleep. She rubbed her
stomach. The slight bulge brought a smile to her
lips before she opened her eyes. Memories of
warm meat flooded her. She felt satisfied. She
wanted to remain like that forever. Content and
filled.

Shuffling feet roused her.

Elisheba was moving about their side of the
tent already.

Miriam sighed. The feeling of contentment
waned out of reach.

She sat up and then lurched. The feeling of
fullness rose in her throat. Her head spun and she
reached up to stop it. She groaned.

"It will help if you move around," her sister-
in-law's voice called nearby.

Moving was the last thing Miriam wanted to do. She laid gently back down and rolled to her side. She pulled her knees up to her chest and wrapped her arms around her legs. The movement was too much and her stomach fought back. She loosened her grip.

"It will pass," Elisheba promised.

Not soon enough. Miriam only thought to herself for fear of opening her mouth. She groaned again.

"I'll get you some water."

She noticed the morning sun fill the room as Elisheba moved the curtain. It left when she returned with the water skin.

"Here." She extended the pouch down to her. "This will help."

Miriam slowly lifted herself onto her elbow so she could drink. She took the skin in her hand and put her lips to the opening. She hesitated. What would happen if she added anything to her already overfilled inside?

"Drink," Elisheba suggested.

She dipped her head back slowly and tried a small sip. The cool water was refreshing to her parched throat, but one small sip was all she was prepared to try. She removed her lips and handed the bottle back to her sister-in-law.

When everything stayed in place, she tried to sit up straight again. The movement was easier this time and she waited for the ache in her midsection to subside before trying another.

"I think you ate that whole bird by yourself."

Miriam's cheeks flushed. She bowed her head.

"I guess I should have cooked another bird."

The image of golden skin and bright white flesh flowed in her mind. Her stomach lurched and she covered her mouth with both hands. If she never looked at another bird again, it would be too soon.

When the ebb of bile subsided, she asked, "There isn't any left is there?"

Elisheba shook her head. "I think you finished it all."

Miriam held her head again. At least she could move about the tent without facing what she knew would trigger a most unwelcome revisit by last night's meal.

She rose to her feet and rummaged through her belongings. A polished bone comb stuck out of her pack. She grabbed it and set to work taming her mane.

When she was happy with the attempt, she reached for her headwrap and set it over her hair. It was then that she noticed Elisheba working something in her hands.

She sat beside her.

Elisheba was turning over something small, thin and white in her hand.

"What is that?" Miriam asked.

"Exactly." The corners of her sister-in-law's mouth turned up.

"What?"

She chuckled. "That's what they call it. 'Manna. What is it.' "

"Call what?"

"This." She grabbed Miriam's hand and turned it palm side up to pour some inside.

Miriam pushed the flakes around with a finger on her free hand. "It looks like frost."

"It covered the ground this morning," she explained.

Moses' words came back to Miriam. He had said something about God raining bread from heaven. But the flakes in her hand didn't look like bread. She had almost forgotten the conversation because of the quail. The thought of the plump bird made her stomach turn over again and she pushed the idea away.

"Manna," her tongue played with the word.

"Moses left a sack for you to gather." Elisheba pointed to the bag. "One omer for every person."

"Is he here?" she stretched toward the curtain that divided the two spaces.

"He and Aaron went out to make sure everyone was gathering for themselves."

"Oh." She eased back.

"I've found it works like grain. I've ground it

together and made some cakes." She retrieved one from a pile and held it out.

Miriam held her stomach. Eating was the last thing she wanted to try.

Elisheba lifted it higher. "Go on."

She reached for the cake and nibbled an edge. It was bland in comparison to the richness of the flesh. The coarse texture was in stark contrast to the smooth flesh that filled her mouth mere hours ago. "It kind of tastes like oil."

"Uh-hun," Elisheba agreed over a bite of her own. "Try it fresh."

She took a pinch off the pile in her hand and dropped the flakes into her mouth. They dissolved quickly. "Tastes like honey." She swallowed. "This was on the ground?"

Elisheba stood. "Moses said we've got to gather it every morning. Well, almost every morning."

Miriam held her head. "I remember something about that."

"Five days we gather our omer," she repeated the instructions. "On the sixth day, we gather twice as much so we don't have to gather on the Sabbath." She brushed the remaining flakes into her sack.

"That should be easy enough to remember."

"Oh," Elisheba said, turning around. "And Moses said we've got to eat it all before we go to sleep. We are not to leave anything for morning." With that, she left the room.

Miriam finished the cake and dusted her hands free of the crumbs. Though the portion of food helped manage her stomachache, she had no desire for any more. She was still too full from the previous night's feast.

She walked into the main area to find Moses.

"Heading out?" he asked.

She nodded.

"Did you gather your portion for the day?"

Her stomach dropped. "I'm not really hungry. I'll gather some later."

"That's not how it works." He shook his head. "You've got to gather it before the sun gets too high."

She tilted her head at him for a moment, but then ducked back to the other side of the tent to retrieve her sack to collect her manna.

Stretching her legs on the short journey felt good. The only problem with a good night's sleep is that her old joints seemed stiff the next morning. She found the place where others were gathering and joined them.

She placed the delicate wafers in her sack until it felt as if the weight was right. The rising sun's heat warmed her back as she gathered. She glanced up to see the sun rising high.

As she went to grab for another piece of

manna, it melted. She stretched her hand to pick up another piece, but it melted too. It was there one moment and then gone the next like frost melting in the heat.

She shook her head at the curious sight.

"An omer?" Moses asked upon her return. He eyed the pouch in her hand.

She nodded and returned the sack to her space. Her stomach was too full to attempt to fill it any more, so she decided to make a few visits around the outskirts.

Miriam dragged her tired feet back to her tent at the end of the long day. She had made many visits. Meeting the needs of so many filled her heart with gladness, but it wore her down as well.

Moses smiled up at her as she entered. "Have a productive day, sister?"

She nodded.

"It's good to see some color in your cheeks," Aaron added.

"It feels good to be serving again." She walked by them. "I'm going to turn in early."

"See you in the morning," Moses called as she passed between the curtains.

Miriam pulled her rolled mat from her pile of things and laid it on a spot on the floor. She smoothed it out as best she could and laid upon it.

Her gaze drifted around the room. They had been sleeping in tents for weeks now, but she still wasn't used to the smell of goat hair surrounding her. The dark color kept the heat of the blazing sun at bay, but it made her ache for the fresh air. She missed taking her mat to the room near the courtyard of their home in Egypt to watch the twinkling stars. She missed the cool breeze on her cheeks that lulled her to sleep.

Her attention landed on the small sack still sitting on the floor next to her things. She sat up and peered inside. Her omer was untouched. She rubbed her midsection as the words of Moses' command in Elisheba's voice came back to her, " 'We are not to leave anything for the morning.' "

She shrugged. "There's no way I can eat all this tonight. What harm could there be?"

She tied up the sack and pushed it aside before she laid down and closed her eyes.

A hustle of movement woke her the following morning. She stretched out on her mat. The ache in her stomach was gone and replaced by fresh hunger. She remembered the bag of manna and reached for it.

She loosed the tie and opened the sack. A foul odor assaulted her nose. "Ew!" She scrambled away.

"What's wrong?" Elisheba entered from the front of the tent.

Miriam crawled to the furthest place in the tent away from the sack. "Worms!" She pointed.

Elisheba peered over the open sack. She waved a hand in front of her nose. "What is that awful smell?"

"It's the manna."

"What?"

"My manna from yesterday."

"You didn't eat it?"

She shook her head. "I wasn't hungry after all the quail. I was away most of the day and didn't come back until nightfall."

Elisheba reached for the sack with outstretched arms and kept her face pointed as far away as she could.

Miriam followed her to the main part of the tent.

"Mariam's portion from yesterday." Her sister-in-law held the bag out for Moses to inspect.

"Is this true?" Moses stared at her.

Miriam looked down. "Yes, but-"

"But nothing. The Lord gave us clear

instructions. We were to leave nothing left for the next day."

"I know. I didn't mean to-"

"Dispose of this." He yanked the bag out of Elisheba's hands and shoved it at her. "Then you need to gather your own omer for today. Hurry the sun is almost fully up."

"Of course." Miriam took the sack and left the tent.

She found a spot on the outskirts of the camp. There she dug a hole and emptied the contents into the sand. Burying it quickly, she turned the sack inside out to let it air out while she walked back toward the camp to collect a fresh omer.

"Were you able to gather your collection?" Moses asked as soon as she was back inside.

She held up the bag.

"Good. Now go eat something."

She brought the sack to her part of the tent.

"I can show you," Elisheba offered.

She nodded.

The two worked in silence for the rest of the morning making cakes.

"You know he's just being hard on you because people watch us," Elisheba offered.

"I know." Miriam hung her shoulders.

"If we are slack in our obedience, what hope does he have for the others to obey?"

Miriam looked up into her sister-in-law's eyes.

"I'll be better."

The next few days, Miriam found herself rising before the sun. She snuck out of the tent with her sack in hand to sit on a rock and watch the manna fall.

Right before the first rays of sun appeared, when the night was stretching back its last grip on the sands, the cloud of God brushed across the land. The delicate wafers appeared all over the ground in its wake.

People emerged from their scattered tents to collect their portion.

She did as well. Day after day she filled her sack until it felt right. Then she returned to her lookout rock and watched the rays melt away what little remained.

On the sixth day, she sat watching the cloud move over the ground. This time, piles formed. Before the cloud had left a thin layer covering the ground. This morning it was twice as big.

She remembered Moses' warnings and set to work collecting twice as much. She watched the people's wide eyes as they too filled their sacks.

When she came into the tent, some of the elders stood around Moses showing him their bags.

He raised a hand to stop them. "This is what the Lord has said, 'Tomorrow is the rest of the holy Sabbath. Bake whatever you need today and store the rest for tomorrow."

"But Moses," one of them inquired. "We tried that the first night. It turned and produced worms."

"I know," he spoke calmly. His sideways glance landed on Miriam for a moment. "Trust the Lord."

Miriam ducked into the women's side of the tent where she found Elisheba baking up a bunch of cakes.

"Do think this will work?" she asked, lifting her bag.

"I guess we will see."

Miriam checked her sack the next morning. The manna cakes she had baked the previous day were still white and fresh as if she picked and baked them that morning. She pushed the sack around from the outside trying to stir any worms that had found their way inside, but there were none. Slowly, she held her nose over the sack and sniffed. No foul odor came from the cakes.

She snuck out of the tent and sat upon her perch.

Sunlight filled the air, but the ground lay empty. The pillar of cloud did not move across the land as it had the past several days.

She saw a handful of people, with sacks in hand, ready to pick their daily portion, but none was found.

"How long are you going to refuse the Lord's command?" Moses' voice boomed beside her. He was addressing those who had gone out to gather. "Don't you see? The Lord has given you the Sabbath. He gave you twice as much yesterday so you didn't have to gather today. Get back to your tents and stay there." He turned toward her.

"Moses, I-"

"Get back to the tent."

She slid off the rock and rushed back to the tent they shared. She didn't stop in the receiving area to speak to Aaron but kept walking to her side of the tent behind the goat hair curtain.

She sat beside her things and pulled her knees up to her chest. Anger and embarrassment raged inside her. She wanted to explain. She wanted to apologize.

Elisheba looked with pity on her as she sat across the tent.

After a few hours, Miriam heard Moses' voice, "Please come in here."

She stood to obey. "Yes, brother." She held her hands behind her back.

"Miriam," he appealed. "I'm sorry I was harsh with you this morning. It angered me to see the people not trusting the Lord. It hurt when I saw you out there too."

"But I wasn't-"

He held up a hand. "I know you weren't out there gathering because you didn't have your sack with you."

Her cheeks grew hot.

He softened. "I wish you could see that your actions have a greater effect than you realize. Our people need leadership and the best leader is one who leads by deed as well as word."

She nodded.

"I'm glad we agree." He smiled. "Now, there is something I need from you."

"Anything."

"Go get your sack of manna and bring it here." He waved toward the curtain. "You too, Aaron."

Their brother rose to obey and Miriam retrieved her sack as well. They laid their bags at his feet.

"The Lord has given a command. Aaron, will you fetch a pot please."

He found a clay pot with a fitted lid and held it out to Moses.

"That will do just fine." He set the pot down in the middle of them. "Now we are each going to put some of our manna in this pot."

Miriam exchanged a glance with Aaron.

Moses took a few handfuls from each of their

sacks until the pot was filled. "The Lord has asked that we put an omer of manna in a pot to keep it for the next generation. They will see the bread that He used to feed us in the wilderness when we left Egypt."

"Won't it stink?" she asked.

Moses shook his head. "The Lord will preserve it as a testimony for all who see it. They will know that the Lord himself provided for us." He placed the lid on top to secure it.

Peace washed fresh over Miriam as she studied the simple container. She had not considered how much God had proven His provision for them since they left Egypt. She thought about the cloud that covered the sands before the manna appeared every morning. It was as if God laid down the manna by hand for His children to gather and eat. They didn't have to hunt. They didn't have to barter with sellers. All they had to do was pick it up.

She remembered the fire that lit their camp at night to keep animals away and provide light.

She thought about the quail from a few nights ago that had not only filled her stomach but revived her spirits. It was at that point she had almost given over to the sorrow and hopelessness that called for her to surrender.

She wiped away a tear and grazed the pot with her fingertips. Its smooth outer layer was cool to the touch.

Thank you, God. She whispered from the depths of her soul. *Forgive me for my disobedience. Help me to become a strong leader for my people.*

Chapter 5

"And all the congregation of the children of Israel journeyed from the wilderness of Sin, after their journeys, according to the commandment of the LORD, and pitched in Rephidim: and there was no water for the people to drink."
-EXODUS 17:1

Miriam set her pack in the fresh sand of their next stop and sat down to remove her sandals. She rubbed her feet, but to her surprise, they didn't ache.

She took a deep breath and evaluated her body. Marching should have taken a lot out of her at her age, but she felt like she could walk another few miles. They had only stopped on Moses' command.

"Where are we?" She looked over at Aaron, who was already unpacking.

He glanced around noticing the placement of distant mountains and the position of the sun. "Rephidim, I think."

A commotion drew their attention. She watched a group of men approach Moses. Their tightened expressions showed focus and resolve. They were not coming for a chat. She could only guess they were coming with more accusations.

"What water are we going to drink?" one questioned.

Moses opened his mouth to speak, but before he could make a sound another added, "Are you going to provide enough for all of us, including our children and cattle?"

"I-" Moses tried again.

"Why did you bring us out of Egypt?" another interjected.

"Everyone is going to die of thirst," the first added.

Many of the men grabbed stones.

Miriam noticed their hands tighten over the rocks.

Moses looked up and raised his arms. "What will I do with these people?" He knelt in the sand. "They are going to stone me."

She watched him listen as his entire body was still with anticipation.

He rose slowly. "The Lord has spoken."

"What did He say?" Aaron asked.

"Gather the elders and get my staff."

Aaron rummaged through the pile of possessions. He handed Moses his rod and rushed off to gather the elders.

Miriam turned to her brother. "What has the Lord said?"

"Come and see."

Moses found a large rock and stood before it. He held his rod high in the air.

The group of men exchanged quiet murmurs.

Moses' arm came down as the wooden staff made contact with the stone.

Vibrations sent shivers through Miriam's body.

The air was silent for a few moments.

Before the murmurings could begin again, the rock shook.

Moses stepped to the side.

Miriam watched as the rock split in two and water flowed from between the opening.

"This place," Moses commanded. "Will be known as Massah because the children of Israel have tempted the Lord."

People came to fill their skins and clay pots as full as they could carry.

Miriam dipped her skin bottle in the free-flowing water. She took a long drink. It wasn't as sweet as the waters in Marah, but it was refreshing and quenched her thirst. She dipped the bottle in the new river again to fill up the pouch for later.

She returned to her possessions and helped set up the tent she shared with her brothers and sister-in-law. Erecting the tent had become easier with practice. It only took half the time to settle everything. She wondered how many more times she would have to assemble the tent.

She looked up at the dark cloth. It was adequate for living in the desert, but she missed her stone home back in Egypt. It had been nice to put in a long day of work caring for the home she shared with her brothers. It was nice knowing exactly where she would lay her head every night. She thought about the cloud that would be outside. It had stopped here. She wondered how long it would stay. They were close to the promised land, yet still so far away.

She sighed.

"Moses, come quick," Aaron's voice strained from the other side of the divided curtain.

Miriam heard their shuffling feet. She followed without a thought.

Her brothers were running toward the border of their camp.

"They came from the north," Aaron explained to Moses as they ran. "We must be too close to their land."

"How many were hurt?"

"Hard to tell." His face whitened. "There was so much chaos."

They came upon a group of injured men.

"Get Joshua," Moses ordered.

Aaron rushed past Miriam.

She stood beside Moses. Looking on the scene sent fear through her heart. She covered her open mouth. "Who were they?" she managed to whisper.

"Amalekites," Moses answered. He pushed his gray hair away from his face. "I thought we had given them enough girth, but it doesn't look like they want us anywhere near their land."

Miriam set to work evaluating the injured men. She sent word to gather bandages and supplies. Some of the midwives came to help.

"Moses," a breathless young man came up behind them.

Miriam finished wrapping the arm of a wounded man when she turned to look upon Joshua. She could see why Eliora blushed when she was in his presence. Though he was less than half Miriam's age, he was handsome by any Hebrew woman's standards. His broad shoulders and chest looked like they could carry the weight of the whole world. His distinguishing features were set flawlessly. If anyone didn't believe in a God who painted beautiful sunsets, all they had to do was look on Joshua's face to see painted perfection.

To top it off, this perfectly sculptured man had a polished inside. Not only was he as humble as any Hebrew man Miriam had met, but he had a strength that seemed to pour from the inside out. He honored God and it overflowed into every ounce of his life. He was close to Eliora's age and the midwife's physical reactions any time he was near betrayed her feelings for the man.

Joshua glanced in her direction as if he could hear her thoughts. She returned her gaze to the man under her hands.

"I need you to choose your best men and fight with the Amalekites," Moses instructed him. "Tomorrow I will stand on top of this hill with my staff."

Miriam glanced over to him at the mention of his staff. *What good would a staff do against such fighting men?*

She finished helping bandage the injured men and left instructions with each to keep their wounds clean and dressed.

She found Moses in their tent. "We have no soldiers."

"Many of our men fought in Pharaoh's army." He folded his arms across his chest and leaned back on a pillow.

"That was in the past. They've had little experience fighting wars out here in the desert."

"Joshua has experience."

"He is far too young to be leading an army."

"The Lord believes he is capable of not only fighting but leading."

She held her breath from releasing her first reply and instead chose another. "I'm not disagreeing with the Lord. I'm simply suggesting that we not pick a fight with people who clearly have the advantage."

"We are not picking a fight with anyone." He huffed. "They attacked first. We have every right to defend ourselves and we match them in people."

"We don't match them in skill."

"That may be true, but we have something they don't."

Miriam raised an eyebrow.

"We have the Lord on our side." He patted the staff which lay beside him.

She eyed the branch. It was becoming like an amulet the Egyptians would wear to bring fortune or favor with their deities. He treated it like his direct line to God.

"I know God is on our side."

"He will fight for us just as He did against the Egyptians."

She met his intense gaze. She'd seen that look before. Their mother's fiery determination mixed with their father's stubbornness. Her heart fluttered at the remembrance of their parents. A deep throb built up inside that longed for their embrace. There was no talking him out of anything with that look in his eyes.

She sighed and let her attention fall back to the stick on the ground. "I'll speak with the midwives. Maybe they will be willing to help. Medically speaking of course."

He inclined his head to the side. "Are you that sure we will lose?"

She shook her head. "I'm that sure if we fight against a trained foe, our people will be hurt."

He pondered the idea for a few moments. "Very well. Go. Speak to the midwives. Seek their aid."

"Thank you, brother." She bowed and left in search of Eliora.

Miriam examined her empty tent and checked with a neighbor. The woman told her the midwife had been called away to assist with a delivery. She gave her directions to the woman's tent.

"Greetings," Miriam called as she found Eliora on the path.

"Greetings." She turned to meet her.

The young woman's bright face and her midwifery bag hung across her body yanked at Miriam's heart. She imagined Puah standing before her instead. She shook away the vision. "I've come to ask for your help."

"Oh?" Eliora advanced a few steps in her direction. She looked ready to run toward the need.

Miriam held up her hands. "Nothing is

wrong."

The midwife eased back on her heels.

"It's for tomorrow."

"Tomorrow?" she wondered.

"I don't know if news has reached you yet about the fighting that went on earlier."

"About the Amalekites?" She nodded. "Some of the women were talking about it. I didn't come to help because of the birth." She pointed over her shoulder at the tent she had just left.

"Of course." Miriam nodded. "Tell a woman, tell the world."

Eliora smiled. "That's what Puah used to say."

Sadness tightened its grip around Miriam's' heart. It had been from Puah whom she learned the saying. She tried to swallow the lump in her throat.

"I might need some help from your guild," she managed to choke out.

"Anything we can do to help."

"Moses is planning an attack tomorrow. I'm afraid there might be injuries. And with your medical training, I was hoping…"

"Say no more." She held up a hand. "I completely understand. I'll have some of my midwives start making preparations right away."

"Thank you."

"Anything for our people."

Miriam relaxed. She still didn't agree with her

brother's plan, but at least she had done what she could to help. She started walking back toward her tent.

"Does Moses believe this is where we are to start staking our claim?" Eliora said, rushing to keep pace beside her.

"What do you mean?"

"Well, when we left Egypt we were told we'd be going to the promised land, right?"

She nodded.

"But the land isn't empty."

Miriam measured the path of her thoughts. "Correct."

"And I don't know much about these people, but I'm pretty sure they won't just leave their land simply because Moses comes calling at their gates."

She considered the evidence. "That's true as well."

"Best I can gather, it's going to come down to a fight."

"A lot of fights." Miriam thought about how vast the land of Canaan was and how many different kinds of people groups occupied the lands.

"A lot of fights," Eliora repeated.

They strode several steps before either one of them spoke again.

"Moses said something about God fighting for

us like He did with the Egyptians," Miriam offered.

"Like the plagues?"

"Or the Red Sea collapsing in on the Egyptian chariots."

Eliora rubbed her arm. "Sometimes, I still hear them chasing us in my dreams."

Miriam fought back the waves of nightmares and visions that waited in the shadows of her mind. She nodded slightly.

"Do you really think God is going to wipe them all out to make room for us?"

"I'm not sure what the actual plan is." She shrugged. "We seem to only get a step at a time."

"And fighting the Amalekites is the next step?"

She shrugged again. "I'm not sure if that step is from God or my brother. Sometimes it's hard to tell."

"Do you think Moses will lead the men well?" she asked.

"He won't be leading them."

The midwife stopped.

She turned back toward her.

"He's going to send those men out into battle without him?"

"He has chosen a captain for the army."

The place between Eliora's eyebrows puckered. "Who?"

"Joshua."

At the mention of his name, Eliora's face changed so drastically, Miriam had to stifle a laugh as not to offend her. The pucker disappeared into a smooth surface. Her pale cheeks flushed so brightly it appeared she had been running laps around the tent city at the hottest part of the day. Her eyes shone with hidden thoughts. The sides of her mouth rose and fell as she tried to shove down the feelings that betrayed her.

"Joshua," his name was a whisper on her lips. She lifted her hands to her face as she tried to rub away the blush that exposed her true feelings.

"He trained with Pharaoh's men," Miriam went on, trying to hide the fact that she could read the struggle going on in the woman. "He did very well there. Moses says the Lord believes he will be a good leader in battle."

"But there are many other men who are older and perhaps wiser in that area." Her cheeks returned to their normal color and the smile of pleasure had left her completely.

"I asked a similar question." She picked up her stride again.

It took a few paces before Eliora caught up with her. "What did he say?"

"He said 'The Lord has chosen,'" she mimicked her brother's deeper tone to lighten the mood.

It worked as Eliora chuckled.

Miriam smiled in return. "In all seriousness, I'm frightened not only for Josh-"

Eliora ducked her head away.

"The men who will fight," she said instead. "But for all our people. That's why I came to request your help."

"There is no question that we will provide aid." She set her gaze ahead.

Miriam caught the edge of resolve in her friend's voice. She knew that it was there because of a certain young soldier, but it was there none the less. For that, she was grateful.

Chapter 6

"So Joshua did as Moses had said to him, and fought with Amalek: and Moses, Aaron, and Hur went up to the top of the hill."
-EXODUS 17:10

"Do we have enough clean linens?" Miriam asked, moving around the newly erected tent on the edge of the camp.

Eliora checked a nearby table. "I've got several piles here ready to go and the others are bringing more."

Miriam looked around at their work. The two had turned the borrowed tent into a station for wounded. They had laid mats around the floor and prepared a place to clean injuries with freshly drawn water. Eliora had sent word to all the midwives to bring clean linens and be available to assist.

With the sun completely up, they were expecting the women at any moment.

"Greetings," a rough voice called from the

entrance.

Miriam turned around in enough time to see Eliora recognize the familiar voice and find something to do on the other side of the tent.

"Greetings, Joshua," Miriam answered. "Are you prepared for today?"

"I am." He nodded. "I was up well before sunrise to pray."

Of course, you were. I'd expect nothing less. She glanced at the newly polished sword that hung at his side.

"It looks like you've done a lot of preparing yourself." He motioned around the tent.

"We are...well..."

He nodded knowingly. "Your brother explained." A bright smile warmed his face. "I think it's a good idea. We've never really done this kind of thing as a people, so we don't know what to expect."

"Joshua?" an older voice called outside the tent.

"If you'll excuse me." He bowed.

"Of course." She returned the gesture.

As he stepped out of the tent, Eliora appeared at her side.

"He's quite handsome," Miriam commented, trying to keep her tone impartial.

"He sure is."

She noticed the midwife's glare was directed

between the flap.

"I mean…" Eliora rung the rag in her hand.

Miriam smirked.

She cleared her throat. "My guild should be here soon."

Miriam glanced through the tent flap where Joshua stood with an older man. "I'll be back in a moment." She stepped outside and came near the men.

"Moses is looking for you on the top of the hill," the older man said.

"I'll go at once." Joshua was off with a long stride.

"Hur?" Miriam called as she came upon the man who was an old family friend.

"Miriam." He reached down to kiss both her cheeks. "It's good to see you."

"And you." She smiled. "Has my brother wrangled you for duty as well?"

"Yes." His eyes shone and then dimmed. "Though not on the battlefield."

"Oh? Then where?"

"On the hill." He pointed off in the distance.

Miriam squinted to see a hill. "Look out?" she guessed.

"Not really."

She tilted her head at him. "I don't understand."

"To be honest, neither do I."

"What is it my brother has asked of you?"

"For Aaron and I to stand on either side of him on the hill and support his arms."

"Now I'm the one who doesn't understand." She closed her eyes and shook her head, trying to force his explanation to make sense. "I thought Moses wasn't going to fight."

"He's not." Hur rubbed the back of his neck. "He said the Lord will fight for us as long as Moses keeps his arms raised."

She pinched the bridge of her nose. "You mean you and Aaron are going to literally support his arms."

He nodded. "That's the plan."

"And what happens if his hands are lowered?"

"We fail." His eyes looked as if they were made of metal.

A group of women came toward the tent. Each had bags slung across their bodies and hands full of supplies.

"May God find favor with you out there," she said to Hur.

"Indeed." He turned and headed toward the distant hill.

"Greetings, ladies," Miriam offered as the midwives approached.

They returned the greeting in a chorus of voices.

"Eliora is inside the tent." She waved behind

her. "Let's get ready for this day."

Soon the tent was busy with quick footsteps.

Eliora had divided the women into groups to help with the flow of events. Some for washing and binding. Others for more extreme medical needs. Still others for passing out food.

Miriam noted how efficient Eliora was and how the women, young and old, yielded under her instructions. She felt guilty for questioning Puah's choice in this woman. It was obvious that she was created to do such work.

"We're ready," Eliora reported to Miriam within what seemed like moments after the group of women arrived.

"Good."

"How long do you think it'll take?" Eliora looked at the flap blowing in the wind.

"I don't know." She looked around the tent at all the women whose eyes were on her. They stood by waiting for instructions and to use their knowledge and talents. "While we wait, let's pray."

Eliora smiled. "I was hoping you'd say that."

Miriam moved to the center of the tent and held onto the center support beam. "Ladies, we are going to pray."

Without further directions, the women moved closer to the center of the tent.

Miriam looked up at the dark ceiling. "God of

the universe, hear our cries to You," she prayed aloud. "Our men have followed You into battle. You have given orders that if they obey, You will provide victory over the enemy. Help them obey. Give my brother, Moses, strength to stand. Give our soldiers…" she paused to look at Eliora before continuing, "…strength to stand in battle. Strengthen their arms. Give them alertness. Give them victory. Thank You for the day You have made."

Eliora nodded in agreement.

The women moved back to their assigned stations and waited in silence.

The stillness had each woman staring at the tent flap.

Miriam felt as if her skin were going to crawl off her body and go charge toward the hill to see what was happening.

A faint sound made its way into the tent. The loud echo of a shofar's call sounded. It was the signal that the battle had begun.

Miriam let out a breath she didn't realize she was holding.

Each woman's attention held fast to the opening. No one spoke. No one moved. It was as if each were a pillar carved from wood and had been left together for storage.

The sun slowly crawled across the sky as the women stood waiting to see if they would be needed at the end of the battle.

"I wish we could know what was happening out there." Eliora's request was almost a whisper in Miriam's ear.

Her heart echoed a plea for safety and victory to the One who was out there with the men.

When the flap was pushed aside for the first time, it was Miriam who greeted the men and pointed them to Eliora.

The one being supported by his fellow soldiers held tight to his abdomen. His lips were pushed back over his gritted teeth.

"What happened?" Eliora asked as she tried to pry his grip loose.

"Sword to the stomach," he panted.

"I need to see it." She fought to pull his fingers free.

"Hurts like fire." He spoke through his closed teeth before lifting his hands just enough for her to peer under them.

"Help me get him over there." She motioned with her chin.

"Of course." Miriam put an arm under the man's elbow and they sidestepped to a station.

"Let's get that tunic off," Eliora instructed. "And get that wound clean."

Women moved around them cleaning and apply oils. They had the wound dressed and the soldier laying on a mat in moments.

"Help!" Two men were dragging in another whose head was bleeding.

"Go." Miriam squeezed Eliora's hand. "I'll sit with him."

Eliora took off.

She reached for a damp rag and wiped the soldiers face. "What's your name?"

"Kishi."

"Mathias' son?"

"That's me," he joked. His body tensed at the pull on his abdomen.

"No joking for at least a week," she tried to sound professional.

"I'll try." He attempted a half smile.

She wiped more dirt off his face. "Can you tell me about the battle?"

"We were doing well at first." He pulled in a ragged breath. "Joshua told us we would if Moses kept his arms up."

Her heart pulled knowing both her brothers were out there and their obedience would determine the outcome. The battle was over if injured soldiers were being removed from the field to be mended, but she didn't know how long before she would see her brothers.

"I remember looking up at the hill and seeing Moses standing there. He had his staff in one hand." He held up his hand as if he was holding a staff himself. "Both hands raised high in the air."

He let his arm fall to his side. "I didn't know who I thought was crazier, Moses or Joshua."

Miriam smiled. *Both.*

"Anyway, we advanced into battle. We were doing well like I said. When things changed, I saw Joshua glance up to the hill. Those were the times Moses had let his hands fall."

She dipped the rag into a bowl of clean water and rung it out.

"One of those times must have been when I got hurt." He pointed to his stomach.

"Rest now. You're in very capable hands."

He closed his eyes.

She stood and moved around the tent. She checked on each station coming back around to where two midwives laid another man they had just finished bandaging.

"What's your name?"

"Nate."

She wiped his dusty face and gave him a sip of fresh water. "Rest," she offered with a pat on his shoulder.

Miriam found Eliora. "How are you holding up?"

The younger woman wiped her bloody hand. "He's the last one that came in." She nodded to the man two women were bandaging. "I had to stitch up his side."

"Will he be alright?"

"Should be. There are several we need to keep an eye on so infections don't set into the wounds."

"Can I help with that?"

"I'd like to keep them here. I know they want to return to their own tents, but I'd feel better if the more serious wounds stay together so we can treat them if signs of infection do arise."

Miriam watched a group of women go from bed to bed with skin bottles of fresh water and manna cakes. "I think they will be better looked after here too."

Eliora nodded and gazed through the tent opening. "Miriam, I wanted to thank you."

"For?"

"For this." She waved around the tent.

"I'm the one who should be thanking you and your midwives. Some of these men might have died without your treatment."

"I mean for giving us the opportunity to serve." She twisted the bloody rag as she cleaned her hand. "Most people just see us as women who help with pregnancies. They don't see all we can do."

"I saw what Puah did for not just our people but all the people affected by the plagues. She stood up in the face of those who thought it better if she had stepped back into the shadows.

"She showed what knowledgeable women are capable of. And she did it not to show off, but to serve. She knew she could help and so she did. She didn't care what others thought about her. She knew her skills could improve… could save lives. She wasn't going to stand by and let that be wasted."

Eliora's eyes glistened. "I miss her so much."

"As do I." She studied her face. "She'd be so proud of you."

Eliora chuckled. "I'll never be half the woman she was."

"Maybe. Maybe not."

She met her gaze.

"But look around at this." She glanced around. "Puah would have been proud of all you accomplished today. She would have jumped right in and helped."

"That's true." She gazed at all the women moving in the tent as if they were following a designed dance. "I'm proud of my guild. They've all worked so hard today."

Miriam followed her glances to every man's face around the tent. She was glad the midwives were not only part of their people but were so willing to use their knowledge to help others.

"Help!" Another group of men carried someone in with them.

Eliora and Miriam both recognized the injured man at once.

The midwife was at Joshua's side in a moment.

"Move him over here," she instructed the other soldiers. She grabbed a sharp knife and sliced his tunic open on the top to reveal his shoulder wound.

The men stood over her watching every movement.

"How can I help?" Miriam asked, moving to her side.

"Get them out of here." She nodded toward the men. "I don't need an audience."

"Of course." She stepped between Eliora and the soldiers who had brought Joshua in. "If you'll excuse us, gentlemen."

"We're not going anywhere." The biggest one stepped forward.

"We need space to work and as you can see we are using up most of it helping the injured." She waved around the tent.

"We're not leaving Joshua," another added, coming to stand behind the first's shoulder.

"I understand your concern," she added. "He is in good hands here. These women are highly trained in medicine. We are doing everything we can to help. What I need from you is to give us the room to do it."

Two of the three left the tent with a huff.

The third still stood by the opening.

"I'm sorry but-" She looked at the one left. "Hur? I didn't see you."

His eyes were set on Joshua.

"He'll be fine," Miriam comforted.

"We did our best to keep Moses' arms up." He slowly moved his gaze to meet her eyes. "My arms were getting so tired. I let them down for just a moment and…"

She reached out and squeezed his shoulder. "Eliora will take care of him."

He nodded.

"The outcome?"

He nodded again ever so slightly. "We gained victory over the Amalekites." He looked around the tent. "But at what cost?"

Miriam followed his gaze. When she turned back to say more, he was gone.

She walked over to Eliora. "How is he?"

The midwife's fingers were working in the open wound. "I don't think any pieces broke off, but I'm double checking." Her gaze was intense as if she were trying to look through his layers of skin and muscle. "Can you have someone bring me some oil?"

Miriam stood and retrieved a pile of clean linens and oil bottle herself.

She set them beside Eliora.

"Thanks." She made another pass in the wound. "I think that will do it."

Joshua gaze darted around.

"Rest," Miriam reassured him. "You are away

from the battle, but you sustained a shoulder wound from an arrow. Eliora is taking care of you." She looked up to see her friend's cheeks flush for only a moment before returning to their normal color.

"Eliora?" he struggled.

Eliora didn't answer. Her focus remained on her task.

"We are going to get you bandaged up."

He opened his lips to speak again, but a wave of pain covered the words with a groan.

"Easy," Miriam ordered. "We're taking care of you."

Joshua relaxed and closed his eyes. His normally olive complexion was pale. Sweat poured from his face.

"We have things for the pain," she offered.

"No," he grunted. "Save it for the others."

Miriam caught Eliora shake her head slightly, but kept her fingers working.

"We have plenty."

"The men," Joshua insisted. He dug his fingers into the ground beside his legs.

"Of course." She dipped a rag into a bowl of water and wiped his brow.

Eliora finished cleaning and dressing his wound.

"I must get back to Moses," he insisted.

"You must rest," Eliora ordered.

Joshua struggled to rise and faltered on his bad arm.

The midwife pressed him back down softly. "Rest."

Joshua slipped into sleep as he laid on the mat.

"Good," she said. "I was about to force some medication on him."

Miriam wiped away a few stray hairs from his sweaty brow.

"I'll sit with them tonight." Eliora settled back on her heels. "Jola has offered to stay with me."

She rose. "I'll come back in the morning."

Eliora nodded, but her attention did not leave Joshua's discomforted face.

"I'll be praying for him," she offered.

The midwife nodded.

Miriam found Moses scribbling on a piece of parchment when she returned to their tent.

"Everyone is tended to," she reported. "Some of the midwives are going to stay for anything that arises through the night."

Moses kept scribing.

"What are you writing there?" She leaned over his parchment.

"The events of today." He continued without looking up.

"You wish to remember it?"

"I wish," he paused and met her gaze. "For Joshua to remember it."

"I don't think anyone will forget a fight like that, especially Joshua."

"It's not just the fight, sister. But we must also remember the One who fought for us."

She nodded. *Thank you, God. Thank You for the midwives who offered aid. Thank You for victory. Thank You for my brothers and the others who help lead Your people. Please continue to guide us and keep Your presence with us.*

Chapter 7

"And Joshua discomfited Amalek and his people
with the edge of the sword."
-EXODUS 17:13

"How did it go last night?" Miriam asked Eliora when she made it to the wounded tent the following morning.

"As long as we can keep the wounds clean, I don't see any problems." The midwife wiped her hand on a rag and looked around the tent. "We've sent most of the men to their own tents to finish their recovery. Only those with serious injuries have remained."

Her gaze landed on Joshua still laying on his mat. "How is he?"

Eliora didn't follow her look. "Better. He still refuses pain management. His wound was pretty deep, but I've been seeing to it personally."

"I would expect nothing less from you."

She ducked her head. "He wants to leave. It's been hard to convince him to stay."

"Let me speak with him."

She nodded and busied her hands with rinsing dirty linens.

Miriam sat on the ground beside Joshua.

He lifted himself onto his good arm.

"Eliora tells me you want to leave our hospitable accommodations," she teased.

"Can I?"

"I'm afraid you suffered a pretty nasty wound. She'd prefer if you stayed here a little longer so she can keep an eye on it."

He looked at the sand.

"It's just that the other men have wives to look after them," Miriam offered. "You are all alone."

His attention came back to her.

"There is no one to take care of you." She motioned to the bandage on his shoulder. The center was a deep crimson.

"I can take care of myself," he insisted.

"Oh, I'm sure you could."

He nodded with a sharp movement of his chin.

"But what happens if your wound gets infected?" she questioned. "What happens if you didn't notice in time and it was so bad that the whole arm had to be removed?"

He didn't meet her full gaze.

"You've seen Pharaoh's men return from war in pieces. Is your pride worth the price of an arm?"

He leaned on his elbow and reached up to rub his injured shoulder. "No," he whispered.

"Then remain here."

He looked up at her, his eyes pleading.

"Just for a few more days until Eliora says you can go home."

"Very well."

"Good." She smiled in victory. "I have something for you."

He perked up some.

She pulled a small pillow out of her shoulder bag.

"What's that?"

"It's a pillow I made from quail feathers from the night God provided for us." Her stomach lurched slightly at the memory. She fought the sensation. "I was hoping it would make you feel more comfortable."

"That's kind of you."

The smile softened on her lips. "May I?"

He stiffened as he adjusted himself to give her room to place the pillow behind his head.

"There."

He laid his head on the soft fabric. "Softer than the hard ground."

She was about to object when she noticed a glint of tease in his eyes. "Now do me a favor."

He tilted his head toward her.

"Get some rest, Captain."

"I'll try." He smiled and eased back into the pillow.

Miriam patted his good arm and return to Eliora's side. "I don't think you'll have any more problems."

The midwife glanced at Joshua and then back at her. "Oh?"

"I set him straight." She winked.

"Thanks."

When Miriam left the tent, she noticed a large group coming toward the direction of their camp. She picked up the hem of her dress and rushed back to her tent.

"Moses," she called.

He met her outside.

"There is a caravan coming from the east."

His attention turned that direction.

"Do you think it's the Amalekites again?"

"They'd be coming from the north." He pointed the other direction.

"Who'd be coming from the east then?"

"I don't know." He turned to her. "Get Aaron and let's go find out."

The three of them made their way to the eastern edge of the tents.

Miriam covered her eyes against the sandstorm that went ahead of the group. "Is that…"

"Father!" Eliezer shouted and ran toward them.

Moses embraced his son. "Greetings."

"Greetings." The young man kissed his

father's cheeks.

Gershom stood beside him and kissed their father too. "It is good to see you well."

"Moses, my son-in-law!" Jethro appeared behind the boys.

"Greetings." Moses kissed the older man's cheeks. "Are you well?"

"I am." He patted him on the back.

"To what do we owe this visit?" Moses enquired as the two men were walked toward the center of the tent city.

"Well," Jethro said. "I've come to return your wife and children."

Zipporah followed a stone's throw behind her father.

Miriam waved to her, but she didn't come any closer. She embraced her nephews.

"I've heard what the Lord has done for the people of Israel," Jethro added.

"He has done a great many things," Moses agreed.

"And I want to hear all about it."

The group made their way to Moses' tent.

Miriam and Elisheba prepared food while Moses recounted the events in Egypt as well as the recent events in the wilderness.

"The Lord has certainly done good unto His people," Jethro commented after the stories were done. "Blessed be the Lord, who has delivered you out of the hands of the Egyptians and out of the hands of Pharaoh. Now I know that the Lord is greater than all gods."

"Indeed," Moses agreed.

"I'd like to make an offering."

"That would be wonderful."

Moses and Aaron took Jethro to the altar, where they made burnt offerings and sacrifices to God. After they were done, Moses saw Jethro and the rest of those with him to his tent for the night.

Zipporah stood on the opposite end of the woman's side of the tent while Elisheba and Miriam cleaned the dishes.

"It's good to have you home," Elisheba said.

She huffed.

"You don't want to be here?" Miriam asked.

"I don't believe I'm welcome."

Miriam exchanged a glance with Elisheba. "What makes you say that?"

"My husband sent us away."

Miriam flinched. "Yes, but-"

"He had no right to send his family away." She threw up her hands. "Do you know how long I've been waiting for word that he was safe? Do you know how many sleepless nights I've had wondering if his neck was under Pharaoh's blade?" Tears streamed down her cheeks.

Elisheba moved to comfort her. "Zipporah-"

"He had no right." She barked again.

Elisheba stepped back.

"We were just sent away like Hagar and Ishmael into the wilderness."

"That's not entirely true," Miriam interjected.

"Sure," she spat. "You'd take your brother's side."

"I'm not taking his side." She straightened. "He sent you away in fear that something would happen to you. He was being used as the instrument of God's plagues on Egypt. He was afraid that Pharaoh would retaliate against his family. Against you."

"You got to stay and Aaron and…" She waved to Elisheba. "You all got to stay while we were sent away."

"He loves you."

"Then why didn't he send for us to return?" Tears streamed faster. "Father heard about your adventures out here in the wilderness and decided to bring us back. Why didn't Moses come get us when you left Egypt? Or at least send for us?"

"I don't know." Miriam reached out to touch her arm.

Zipporah pulled away.

"But I do know he loves you and those boys more than his own life."

She huffed again.

"Maybe he was waiting until we got settled in Canaan before he sent for you," she tried. "At least being with your father and your people he knew you'd be safe from harm."

She wiped her face with the back of her sleeve.

"He does love you," Elisheba added.

"Has our name crossed his lips since you've been free?"

Miriam and Elisheba exchanged another glance.

"I thought so." She turned away from them and laid down in the furthest corner of the tent, keeping her back to them.

Elisheba looked helplessly into Miriam's eyes.

"Give her time," Miriam whispered. "Some wounds take longer to heal."

Miriam found Moses sitting in a high place early the next morning. People had lined up for him to judge their disputes. It had become a common sight.

Jethro came to stand near her. "He does this every day?"

"Most days." She nodded.

"That doesn't give him much time to do anything else."

Miriam simply glanced back to her brother.

"How can he lead when he has to spend all of

his time listening to common grumbles?"

She shrugged. "What else is there?"

Caleb and another young man flanked Moses on either side. The men had insisted on being nearby as protection. People's arguments could get heated.

Miriam shook her head and walked away. She didn't want to waste a perfectly good day standing around listening to complaints even if her brother did.

She found Eliora in the borrowed tent at the edge of their makeshift city. Only two men remained under her care.

"How are they today?" Miriam asked when she entered the tent.

"Both are well enough to leave today," she answered, ringing out a cloth. "I was going to start disassembling the tent as soon as I finished their fresh bandages."

"I'll help."

"Are you sure your brothers can spare you?"

She nodded a tired agreement. "I don't think I'm built to listen to arguments. Moses gets more worn with each passing day."

Miriam went to check on the two men. The first was an older man who had little family to help. His wound was healing as well as could be expected.

Eliora finished his bandage and sent him to his

own tent with a promise to check on him in a day or so.

The last man left was Joshua. He was sitting up in a corner of the tent packing a bag with his free hand.

"Let me help with that," Miriam said, joining him.

"Thanks."

"I bet you're excited to return to your own tent." She folded a blanket and placed it in the open sack.

He nodded. "More than you know."

Though it was covered by a new tunic, Miriam could see the top of Joshua's bandage over his right shoulder. Eliora had cleared him to return to his duties as long as he took care of himself and notified her of any complications.

"Oh." He reached behind himself. "This is yours." He handed her the small, quail-feather pillow. "Thanks for allowing me to borrow it."

"I'm glad it brought some comfort." She accepted the pillow and set it next to herself.

"I think that's all my stuff." He put the strap on his good shoulder.

They rose in the same movement.

"Moses is still at the hill as judge if you want to go back to your duty."

"Thanks again," he replied with a warm smile.

Eliora's gaze followed him out of the tent.

"I wish there were a lot more of him in this congregation," Miriam commented when he was out of sight.

"Me too."

Miriam's chuckle snapped Eliora from her glare.

"Let's get this tent taken down."

When no more remained of the healing tent, Miriam returned to her own tent to find her brother in an intense discussion with Jethro.

"What are you doing?" Jethro huffed. "Why do you sit alone and listen to the people's problems from sunrise to sunset?"

She fingered the edges of her pillow, wondering if she would be welcome to stay and participate in the discussion or if she should move on.

"Because the people come to me to ask of the Lord," Moses explained simply. "I assist them when they have a disagreement they can't settle alone and I help them remember the laws of God."

"This is not a good thing."

Moses perked up.

"You are going to wear away."

Miriam silently agreed.

"Both you and these people. This thing is too heavy for you and you are not able to perform it alone."

Moses pulled his shoulder's back to sit a little

straighter.

Miriam noticed he looked like he was going to argue, but hesitated as his father-in-law's words sunk into his mind.

"Hear me," Jethro continued not waiting for Moses to defend himself. "You have men you trust?"

He nodded, trying to follow the path of his father-in-law's thoughts.

"Teach the people the ordinances and laws and show them how to walk with God and what they must do. Then set over them able men who fear God, men of truth who hate covetousness. Divide them into groups. Set some over thousands, some over hundreds, others over fifties, and yet others over tens."

Moses' eyes shone with the idea and his hand came up to smooth out his beard.

"Let them judge the people. If there should come a great matter that they can't handle, then it can be brought to you to judge. This way the burden will be spread over multiple shoulders and you will not carry it alone."

As if a physical weight had been lifted, Moses' shoulders straightened even more. "That is wise counsel."

"Indeed." He nodded, seemingly pleased with his own idea. "This way you and the people will endure and live in peace."

The next morning, Moses called on men from all tribes to gather at the place he sat and set to work dividing the people among them.

Right before midday, Jethro met Moses and the rest of his family outside their tent.

Miriam noticed Moses' bright smile and lifted steps.

"I feel like a great burden has been lifted," Moses explained. "The thought of the people's needs still being met while I enjoy an afternoon is so freeing."

"May God continue to bless you," Jethro smiled and embraced Moses.

"And you as well."

Miriam hugged Jethro's neck. "I'm grateful to you," she whispered in his ear.

"We all need a little wise counsel in our lives," he whispered back. "Take care of your brother."

She rubbed her face in his bushy beard. "Of course."

He pulled her back to arm's length. "This is where we part."

She nodded and pulled him in for another hug. "Thank you for bringing his family back."

"Though I enjoyed spending time with my

grandsons, they need to be with their father. Their years are passing fast and they need his guidance. And Zipporah..." His eyes lost a little brightness at his daughter's name.

"Elisheba and I will look after her," she promised.

"May God continue to bless your journey."

"May God bless your return home." She kissed his cheeks and waved him off.

Chapter 8

"For they were departed from Rephidim, and were come to the desert of Sinai, and had pitched in the wilderness; and there Israel camped before the mount."
-EXODUS 19:2

"So that's the mountain?" Miriam asked, pointing up with her chin.

Moses nodded. "That's it."

She stood staring up at Mount Sinai. It had taken the people sixteen days to travel there. Moses spoke constantly to them about the mountain where God was leading them.

She tilted her head. The mountain looked like any other hill they had passed in the desert. It was larger than most of the others, but composed of the same sand and rocks. Nothing distinct jumped out at her.

"Set up the tent," he asked as he set down his load. "I've got to go meet with the Lord."

Miriam set down her pack. She stretched her

back and started opening the bags. With as many times as they had set up and tore down the same tent, she figured she could probably set it up in her sleep.

She watched her brother's form disappear toward the mountain.

"What do you think God will have to say?" Elisheba asked, coming over to help.

"I don't know, but we will all find out soon enough."

The tents had been set in order and the final details put in place by the time the sun was low in the sky.

Moses came in and called for Aaron.

"Here, brother," Aaron answered.

"We need to gather the people," he said. "I have much to tell them."

It wasn't long before Moses stood high on a cliff of the mountain above the people.

"The Lord has spoken," he started, his voice deep and echoing over the crowd. "He has said, 'You have seen what I did unto the Egyptians. How I carried you on eagle's wings and brought you unto myself. Now, if you obey my voice and keep my covenant, then you will be a treasure unto me above all people. You will be a kingdom of priests unto me. A holy nation.' "

Miriam let the words flood her soul. The familiar wash of peace, which only came from the movement of God, rushed over her. She closed her eyes and imagined the people around her bright and shining. Moses' words conjured a picture of a glorious people serving God with their whole being. The thought filled her with such contentment that it brought the corners of her mouth up.

"All that the Lord has spoken we will do," the people agreed in unison.

"The Lord has said, 'I come unto you in a thick cloud as a sign that I am speaking.' " Moses looked out over the group. "He has asked that today and tomorrow we wash our clothes and prepare ourselves. For on the third day, the Lord will come down in the sight of all of you on this mount. We will set boundaries around the mountain. Be warned," he cautioned and raised both arms. "Do not go up into the mountain or touch the border of it. Whoever touches the mount will surely be put to death. Neither beast nor man may touch the mountain." He let the severity of the warning hang in the air before he turned and headed back down to the people.

"See to it a border is established immediately," Moses instructed Joshua.

He bowed deeply and set to work.

"Miriam," Moses called.

"Brother?"

"I want you to check on the widows and such.

Make sure they have what they need to prepare themselves."

"Of course," she answered.

"I want all people to be able to obey."

For the next two days, Miriam went from tent to tent checking on those who lacked. She helped fetch water for those who could not and scrubbed elbow deep with those whose hands were too weak to wash.

On the third day, the people stood once again before the mountain. The boundary had been finished and people kept their distance.

A thick cloud descended to cover the top of the mountain. Flashes of lightning and rolls of booming thunder came from the cloud. Pillars of smoke mixed with the thick cloud and the mountain quaked.

Miriam's knees trembled at the sight and sound. She wasn't alone. Many people stepped back from the mountain. Some covered their faces or bowed to the ground. There was no doubt in her mind that the cloud was the presence of God. It was strangely familiar. It called to her to come near and yet was distinctly separate from her as a warning to stay away.

"I don't know if the mountain is strong enough to withstand the presence of God," Miriam whispered to Eliora who had joined her side near the front of the congregation.

A piercing sound, long and loud, peeled from the cloud.

"It sounds like trumpets calling," Miriam remarked. "How can that be when no one is there to blow them?"

Moses headed toward the mount.

She grabbed his arm. "Where do you think you're going?"

"God is calling. I must go."

The resounding trumpet-like call sounded again even louder.

"You can't go up there," she protested. "The mount shakes before the cloud. How will you be able to stand?"

"God calls." He patted her arm and faced the mountain again. "I must go."

She released him.

As she watched his figure climb higher into the thick cloud, the press around her became strong. Many of the people crowded around her near the boundary.

Moses suddenly appeared on a cliff that jutted out from the mountain. "Please, remain back," he ordered and pushed his hands out. "The Lord doesn't want any to perish because of your curiosity." He waved his hands out again as if he could push the multitude and force their obedience. "Aaron," he waved his brother forward.

He took a careful step closer.

"The Lord has called for you and me to go up into the cloud."

Aaron was only a few steps from the boundary. He looked up at his brother.

"You will be well," Moses encouraged. "The Lord has asked for you to join me."

He looked back at Miriam before stepping over the freshly dug ditch. He climbed up to where Moses stood and the two continued the journey further up the mountain together.

Miriam took a step closer. Curiosity ruled her compulsion. She wanted to join the meeting. She wanted to face the feeling that led her from the inside out.

Moses and Aaron had been called. But she was like them. How come she couldn't go up the mountain? Surely if her two brothers could make the climb, so could she. She was a prophetess. She was a leader. She edged her toes closer to the limit. One more step and she would be close enough to cross the barrier.

A flash of lightning peeled and a clap of thunder sounded. The fearful sight made her take several steps back as if the warning had been personally for her.

Her heart beat faster. Her hands flew up to her chest. She took a few breaths to steady herself. She looked up to the thick cloud hiding the top of the mountain. Smoke pillars plumed upward and streaks of lightning stretched out like fingers. If God was warning her to stay back, she wasn't going to be the one to test His mercy today.

It wasn't long before Miriam saw the forms of her brothers climbing down the mountain. They met the people at the cliff where Moses could speak and his voice would carry over the gathering.

"I have word from the Lord," he called.

Aaron stood by his side.

"The Lord has given commands for us to follow. Hear Israel what the Lord has said, 'You will have no other gods before Me. You will not make any carved image or likeness of anything that is in heaven or earth or sea. You will not bow yourself down to them in worship. I am the Lord your God and am a jealous God. I will visit the iniquity of the father to his children for up to four generations. I will show mercy unto thousands of them that love Me and keep My commandments.' "

He took a breath before continuing, " 'You will not take the name of the Lord in vain. Remember the Sabbath and keep it holy. Honor your father and mother that your days will be long upon the land which I have given you. You will not kill. You will not commit adultery. You will not steal. You will not bear a false witness. You will not covet anything your neighbor has.' "

"All the words which the Lord has spoken will we do," the gathering shouted together.

Chapter 9

"And the LORD said unto Moses, 'Lo, I come unto thee in a thick cloud, that the people may hear when I speak with thee, and believe thee for ever.' And Moses told the words of the people unto the LORD."
-EXODUS 19:9

Miriam rose early to find her brothers hard at work at the foot of the mountain.

Moses directed men in the construction of pillars.

"What's all this?" she asked.

"Altars to the Lord," he explained. "One for each of the twelve tribes." He counted off each in turn. "The Lord has asked for a sacrifice to confirm our agreement to the covenant."

Moses had the young men make burnt and peace offerings to the Lord when the altars were complete. He held some of the blood back along with the parchments he had written on the night before. He took them up to the ledge and read aloud the same commandments again.

The people responded, "All that the Lord has spoken will we do."

He dipped a branch in the bowl and flung it out over the people and the parchments.

Dots of red spotted the clothing of everyone around Miriam. She looked down to see her freshly cleaned dress covered with tiny spots of ox blood.

"Behold," Moses words caught her attention. "The blood of the covenant which the Lord has made with you concerning all these words."

Miriam met her brother when he returned with the parchments and empty bowls.

"What's the next step?" she asked. "Are we heading to Canaan now?"

He returned the bowls to Aaron. "Walk with me, sister."

She kept his unhurried pace for some time.

"The Lord has called us back up the mount." He didn't allow his gaze to fall on her.

"Who?"

"Myself, Aaron, Nadab, Abihu, and several others."

"You're going back up there?"

"The Lord has called."

"How many more times will you return to the cloud?"

"As many times as the Lord calls," he answered

simply.

She remained quiet for several more steps. Her thoughts hastened over the explanation. "How many more will He call up?"

Moses paused and turned to face her.

She could see questions flash in his eyes. She wondered if she should ask the one that she concealed deep in her heart.

"It's not up to us who the Lord calls."

"But if He did call someone else…" She hesitated to add her name to the list.

"Then I would bring them up."

Her heart skipped a beat. She thought of the mystery that laid hidden behind the cloud. *Could Moses really see the true presence of God? Had Aaron?*

"For now." Moses picked up his stride. "The Lord has called the elders to come up with me."

They reached their family tent.

Moses secured his spotted parchments among his possessions. "How are the widows?"

"Well." Miriam watched his smooth movements around the tent. "There are many who need aid. I was thinking about asking the midwives for help."

"I wanted to thank them for assisting with the injured soldiers." He rubbed his beard. "I know they were simply using their talents to offer support when it was needed, but I'd like to show my appreciation."

"The women are humble." She shrugged. "They do their work for the pleasure of service, not accolades."

"I see." He finished putting away his materials and turned to head out of the tent.

Miriam followed.

"Still, I think something should be done."

"Perhaps a small feast?" she offered.

Moses hummed as he thought over her suggestion.

"A way to show them you recognized how hard they worked."

"I like it." He wrapped his massive arm around her shoulders. "Set things in order and we shall feast in their honor."

They reached the bottom of the mountain, where the group of men was gathered with Aaron.

Moses removed his arm from her shoulder and started the climb.

Miriam watched as man after man crossed the barrier, climbed the rocks toward the top, and was eventually covered by the cloud.

Her toes came close to the boundary. She glanced up. The welcomed climbers had gone from Moses to Aaron and now expanded to over seventy other men. *Why aren't I counted among them? What could be so special about them that I'm not welcome to come any closer than the bottom of the mountain?*

A clap of warning thunder pushed her back. She walked to her tent alone and found the place empty.

She retrieved her timbrel. Her fingers brushed the tight skin. She beat her palm a few times, setting a pulse. Words flowed from her lips in a simple song.

She sighed and went back to rubbing the worn places on the instrument.

When she held her instrument, she usually felt connected to God. She thought of Moses' rod and understood why he prized it so. It was his connection to God just as her timbrel was hers. She pulled the instrument close to her chest. Tears burned at the corners of her eyes.

She pulled the timbrel away and placed it on her lap. Her heart longed to sing praises, but something was in the way. She thought about the cloud over the mountain. She imagined what it would be like to cross the border and see what the men had been invited to observe. Her heart ached. She wanted to be close to God.

I am here. The quiet voice whispered within.

Her hands trembled as they tightened on the round edges of her timbrel.

"God?" She looked around hesitantly.

No answer came, but peace enveloped her.

"I'm sorry." She closed her eyes and let the

tears flow. "I want so much to be like my brothers. To be welcomed in your presence."

I am here.

She smiled and opened her eyes. Lifting her timbrel, she patted out a steady beat while a fresh song danced over her tongue. A song of praise. A song of repentance.

Miriam worked the rest of the day with many of the other women in the camp to organize a feast for the midwives. Everyone pulled together a worthy meal.

The men returned from the mountain just in time to join them.

"You've done well, sister." Moses gave a pleasing gaze over the gathering.

She blushed. "I wanted to show them how much I appreciated them too."

He studied her for a few moments. "You seem better."

She nodded, then studied his demeanor as well. "You seem different too."

"We have much to share." His smile widened. "Let us feast."

After a simple blessing and encouraging words on behalf of the honored guests, Moses invited the people to enjoy the festivities.

Miriam filled her plate and sat with her brothers to listen to their stories from the mount. "What did you see?"

Moses' eyes shone. "It was the most incredible sight I've ever seen. The God of Israel was right there above us." He waved his hands above his head for emphasis. "Under His feet was a paved work that appeared to be a pure sapphire stone."

"What did God say?"

"He gave Moses more instructions," Aaron added "Then he told him to come back with Joshua tomorrow and He would give him three tables of stone with the commandments written on them."

"Joshua?" Miriam protested. "He's barely more than a boy."

"What has gotten you so worked up?" Aaron tried to calm her with a hushed tone. "This is what God had said."

Miriam could feel heat rising in her cheeks. She closed her eyes and focused on her breaths. When she opened her eyes again, Aaron was still staring at her.

"Forget it." She rose and found something to busy her hands.

Miriam hauled her tired body back to her tent when the feast was over and cleaned up. With an exaggerated movement, she pulled out her mat and unrolled it. Elisheba and Zipporah were already sound asleep on their own mats. She yawned and stretched.

Within moments of closing her eyes, images of

lightning sweeping down the mountain invaded her dreams. Screams surrounded her. She searched for their source. It took several minutes before she realized she was the one screaming.

She had found herself on the wrong side of the boundary line. Lightning reached down and touched her skin. Burns left lightning marks all over her arms. She rubbed them to try to put out the burning sensation.

She woke up screaming to the pale light just before dawn. With a quick glance around her, she realized she was alone in the tent. She looked down at her arms. Her olive complexion only marked with age glared back at her. She breathed a sigh of relief.

She rose and hurried to meet the group at the foot of the mountain.

Moses was standing with Joshua, Aaron, Hur, and many of the others.

"Wait here for us," Moses instructed the elders. "Joshua and I are going up the hill alone. If anyone has any dispute that cannot be handled, take them to Aaron or Hur." He waved to his brother and friend. "Let them judge the matter."

Aaron and Hur nodded in unison.

Moses waved them off and climbed with Joshua fresh on his heels.

Miriam watched them disappear into the cloud. Her arms tingled when she saw a few strikes of lightning. She looked down to check her skin though she found none of the marks that had been in her dream.

"They're heading up again?" Eliora stood near her.

She turned toward her friend and gave a simple nod.

"Why isn't Aaron going with them?" She motioned with her chin toward Miriam's brother who was heading back to camp with the elders.

She shrugged. "Moses said only he and Joshua would be making this trip."

"Joshua?" The midwife's eyes widened.

She hesitated with what words to offer as comfort.

"Why Joshua?"

"Moses said he'll be training him to help lead."

"It isn't enough that he leads the warriors?" Her eyes flamed. "He must be second in command now as well?"

"Moses thinks-"

" 'Moses thinks,' " she mocked. "I'm growing tired of constantly listening to Moses."

Miriam held her tongue and waited until her anger passed.

Eliora finally met her gaze. She hung her head. "I'm sorry."

"I know you're worried about him," she offered, with a tight grip on her friend's arm.

"Moses is following God."

"I know." The midwife lifted her head slightly. "I just don't want to see any more harm come to him."

Miriam remembered the blood-soaked shoulder bandage that stood a testimony of the last time Joshua had followed Moses' plan. She reached over and wiped away a few loose strands of hair from her friend's face. "God has called them. He must go."

Chapter 10

"And Aaron said unto them, 'Break off the golden earrings, which are in the ears of your wives, of your sons, and of your daughters, and bring them unto me.' "
-EXODUS 32:2

Miriam stood staring up at the cloud-covered mountain. It had been over a month since she had seen any movement besides lightning strikes and smoke pillars. There had been no sign of Moses or Joshua.

Eliora stood a few feet behind her.

She twisted over her shoulder to see the fearful eyes of her friend watching the cloud too. Miriam reached for her.

The midwife turned on her heels and fled to the camp.

Miriam sighed and return to her own tent to find Aaron sitting in the open area.

"Still no sign of them?" he asked.

She glanced at him for a brief moment to see

his attention was on the open tent flap as if he could see all the way to the mountain. "No."

"Aaron," a male voice called from outside.

Both siblings turned to the sound.

"Enter," Aaron called.

A group of men filled the area.

"Yes?" Aaron asked.

"Will Moses be returning?" asked the appointed leader who stood a full head height above the others.

Aaron's attention went back momentarily to the flap before answering, "I'm not sure."

"It's been forty days," the man's voice had an edge that Miriam couldn't place.

"I know." He hung his head.

"Maybe we should go on without him," the man suggested.

Aaron met the man's pleading gaze, but didn't answer.

"No," Miriam intervened. "Moses gave us instructions to wait for his return."

"What if he doesn't come back?" the man inquired what they had all been thinking. "What if something has happened up there? How would we know?"

Miriam squared her shoulders and stood between the group and her brother. "We will wait."

"Aaron?" the man looked around her to where

her brother still sat.

He didn't answer.

"Up!" the man yelled and took a step forward. "Make us gods to go before us back to Egypt. Moses brought us out, but we don't know what has become of him."

Miriam spun around to face her brother. She held her tongue, but pleaded with her eyes.

He only looked at her for a moment and then stood. He passed her to stand in front of the men. "Break off the golden earrings which are in the ears of your wives and of your children." He hesitated. "Bring them to me."

The men left the tent.

"Aaron, what are you doing?" Miriam interrogated.

He sighed. "They're right."

"They most certainly are not." She shook her head.

"We don't know what happened to Moses."

"He's in the cloud on the mountain." She pointed to the open flap.

"He's never been gone this long."

"He'll come back."

"And if he doesn't?" Aaron met her gaze and held it.

She searched her thoughts. Nothing came forward as an alternative solution. "I…," she wavered. Her gaze met the sandy floor. "I don't know."

"It's been too long. Moses left me in charge-"

"You *and* Hur," she corrected. "Maybe you should seek his counsel."

"I don't need anyone else's counsel." He left the tent.

She longed for Moses. His wisdom-filled words would set all this right. Of course, if he were there to give them, they wouldn't be having the discussion.

She pushed back the tent flap and followed Aaron to the gathering place near the foot of the mountain.

Men from every tribe brought forth handfuls of gold earrings to Aaron. He set to work melting down the metal and fashioning them together. Before sunset, a golden calf stood among them.

Miriam looked on the striking thing. Aaron's skill had formed a beautiful piece of craftsmanship. It's outside shone in the dying rays of sun. He had polished it to perfection.

"This is a representation of your god, Israel," Aaron called out to the people. "The god that brought you out of Egypt."

A loud clap of thunder sounded as if in response to his claim, but none of the people responded. The sound had become too familiar to the others over the last month.

Miriam's skin tingled. The faint memory of

the burning dream flashed in her mind. The sound brought fear and warning with it. She feared what her brother had done. *Where are you, Moses?*

"Let us build an altar to our god." Aaron reached for a stone and started a foundation around the calf.

Others pitched in to help until an altar formed a perfect circle around the statue.

"Tomorrow we will feast," Aaron proclaimed.

The crowd cheered.

Miriam held her breath. Her skin burned as she gazed upon the stormy cloud above the mountain.

"Aaron." She tugged her brother's sleeve as the crowd dispersed. "What are you doing?"

"See." He pointed to the calf. "I've created a god to lead us back."

"To Egypt?"

He nodded. "To Egypt."

"I don't want to go back to Egypt," she whimpered. "I want to go to Canaan."

"Moses is gone." He ripped his sleeve from her hand. "And I don't intend to start a war with the Canaanites."

"But all the things God did to bring us out of Egypt and into freedom-"

"Were all well and good until we were left leaderless." He looked to the shining calf. "We have our god now and we are heading back to

Egypt." He turned and left her standing alone.

Her gazed lingered over the golden calf. Its smirk seemed to mock her. Her lungs burned with lack of breath and her chest tightened. She hated all this. She wanted Moses back. She wanted to see her people go forward, not backward.

What had all the plagues been for if not to fully release us from Egypt's grip? she prayed. *Why have You provided each step away from slavery? Why have you seemed to leave us alone in the desert without guidance? Please bring my brother back, God.*

Miriam dragged herself to the calf earlier in the morning than she would have liked. She wanted to stay in her tent and as far away from the madness as possible. Yet her brother had ordered everyone up before sunrise to witness the offerings.

Once the burnt and peace offerings were made, the dedication of the statue was completed.

"Let us eat," Aaron ordered.

The people sat together and shared all the food they could find.

Miriam sat next to Eliora though she didn't add to the conversation.

When everyone had their fill of food, Aaron

stood over them.

"Now, let us rise and play." His smile was mischievous as he led them away.

"Play?" Miriam questioned, but Aaron had walked too far to hear her.

She turned to Eliora. "What does he mean by that?"

The midwife shrugged.

Aaron led the group out to the open field where the calf shone bright on its altar.

Miriam looked up the cloud covered mountain. She squinted trying to catch the slightest glimpse of Moses' form descending, but saw nothing. She sighed and turned her attention back to Aaron.

He lifted his voice to sing.

The people around her joined him and some danced around the altar.

Her attention returned to the mountain. The thunders roared and bolts of lightning flashed, but no one else turned their attention to it. They were too distracted by their folly.

"Grab your timbrel, sister," Aaron called as he danced by.

She shook her head.

People whirled around her. Her heart raced as the nightmare haunted her. Some removed their clothing. Whether from the heat of dancing or the madness of mind, she couldn't tell. All she knew is she didn't want to be anywhere near the golden calf.

She picked up the hem of her tan dress and ran toward her tent. Once inside, she held herself in a tight hug. She tried to calm her ragged breath and rapid heart.

When she could breathe comfortably again, she relaxed and gazed around the tent. Her timbrel sat on its side against her bag. She reached for it and brought it to her lap. Her fingers tightened on the wooden edge.

She brushed her fingertips over the worn skin. Her palm had worn a place in the skin over the years. She remembered the day she first held the instrument. A neighbor in Egypt was a master carver. His specialty was instruments.

It was under his guidance that she formed the outer circle of wood to hold the skin tightly in place. He even showed her how to pound it just the right way to produce the sounds she wanted. It wasn't long before she had mastered every inch of the instrument.

This was the same timbrel she used to praise God on this side of the Red Sea. Their first night of freedom from Egypt had sparked a song of celebration. She helped lead the praise with her brothers.

Moses' face filled her mind.

Oh, Moses. Where are you?

The sound of singing filled the air around her.

Tears blurred her vision. She pulled the timbrel close to her chest.

"Moses," she repeated his name as a whisper on her lips.

She pulled the instrument back again and ran her fingertips over the worn skin. Thoughts of Egypt filled her mind. The men had asked Aaron for a god to lead them back to Egypt. The golden calf made her skin shudder. They had created a form to represent God. Aaron had been careful not to call it God, but a god.

Miriam remembered the statues in Egypt. The people had created almost every animal to represent their gods. They carved every form of the mortal to represent the immortal. They offered sacrifices… sacrifices just as Aaron had done for the calf. They had special feasts, just as Aaron had given earlier. They worshiped the idols… idols. Aaron had created an idol.

The tears in her eyes spilled out onto her cheeks and stained the skin of her timbrel. Her instrument was for the praise of God, not some statue pretending to be Him.

She wiped her face with the back of her sleeve and set her timbrel back in its place. She rose and left the tent. She didn't know where to go, but couldn't bring herself to go back to the field at the foot of the mountain. She wouldn't look on the display of folly.

She heard voices a few steps away and her curiosity drew her near.

A group of people stood together.

She recognized Caleb, son of Jephunneh, in the midst of them. He was an aid to Moses, like Joshua. He was listening to the group's concerns. The others were familiar as well. She recognized each of the faces of her nephews, cousins, and other relatives.

"This isn't right," Eleazar pleaded.

"I'm in agreement with you," Caleb said as he extended a hand and placed it on the man's shoulder. "I'm simply trying to figure out a way to get to Aaron and talk some sense into him."

"Did you see those people?" her nephew, Ithamar, asked.

Caleb nodded solemnly.

"They made themselves naked before that thing," her other nephew, Eleazar, continued.

Miriam watched a shudder run through him. Her own body shook at the sweeping images of bare-skinned people dancing before the makeshift altar.

She stepped closer.

The men turned at her advance.

"Aunt Miriam?" Eleazar approached her. "What are you doing?"

"I couldn't stay…" she tried to explain, but her

voice broke.

He reached out and pulled her in close. "I know." He held her out to arm's length. "We are working on a plan to stop them," he promised.

She tried to smile, but tears burned her eyes.

"How could they…" her voice betrayed her again.

He looked over her head at Caleb. "I don't know."

Caleb glanced in the direction of the singing.

"Why don't you go to my tent," Eleazar offered. "The other women have gathered there to stay out of the field."

She nodded.

"Let them know we will return as soon as we have a plan," Ithamar added.

"Of course." She made her way cautiously through the nearby tents. She kept her gaze on the sand so she wouldn't accidentally look upon the people's disgrace.

When she found Eleazar's tent, she pushed the flap open.

Several heads turned her direction as she entered.

"Miriam." Elisheba rushed to embrace her. "I'm so glad you're here." She kissed her cheeks.

"Peace," she said. "I'm well."

"Can you believe what's going on out there?" she asked, as she put her arm through Miriam's and led her deeper into the tent. "It seems our tribe is the only one not swayed." She waved around.

Miriam noted the observance. Every woman there belonged to the tribe of Levi by birth or marriage. She didn't see anyone missing.

"I met the men on the way." She patted her sister-in-law's arm. "They were with Caleb making a plan to stop this."

Her eyes searched each face. The bits of hope were broken and curious at the mention of Caleb's name. She noticed one face that didn't meet hers.

Zipporah sat in the corner of the tent with her back turned away from everyone else.

"Have you still not forgiven your husband?" Miriam asked, coming to sit beside her.

A swift look of disdain was her only answer.

"You are here now with your sons," Miriam tried.

"Once again without my husband," her voice broke through her guarded barrier.

Miriam caught a red rim around her eyes. "He will return."

"Just as he did for his family?" she barked and then turned herself away again.

Miriam stretched a hand to place it on her sister-in-law's shoulder, but she hesitated. She didn't have any words of comfort or explanation for Moses' behavior. He was doing what he felt the

Lord calling him to do. Yet it often brought pain and confusion to others.

"I'm not giving up on him." She whispered. Whether to Zipporah or herself, she wasn't sure who needed to hear it more.

Chapter 11

"And the LORD said unto Moses, 'I have seen this people, and, behold, it is a stiffnecked people:' "
-EXODUS 32:9

The Levite men returned to the tent to check on the women within the hour.

"What news do you have?" Miriam asked Caleb.

"Nothing much has changed," he reported. "The noise continues. We have decided a group of us are going to confront Aaron. The rest will remain here until this is over."

"Maybe I should go," she offered.

Caleb shook his head and opened his mouth to speak.

"He's my brother," she interrupted. "He'll listen to me."

"I wish Joshua were here." He hung his head. "He always knows what to do."

Miriam waited.

"I don't think it's a good idea to put you in the

path of temptation." He looked back at her. "We can handle speaking with Aaron."

"You might be able to speak," she replied. "But I can get him to listen."

"If you think it will help."

She set her shoulders. "Lead the way."

The small group headed toward the open field.

Miriam stayed behind Caleb's massive frame. He was about the same age as Joshua and just as ruggedly built. She kept her glare on his sandals hoping to spare her eyes from any further indecency.

It wasn't long before Caleb stopped.

She wanted to dare a peek around him, but the continued shouts and song warned her that the celebration had still not died down.

"Aaron," Caleb called.

Miriam fought the urge to look up again. She closed her eyes.

"Aaron!" His deep voice boomed.

"Ah! Finally decided to join us?" Aaron's joyous voice rung somewhere nearby.

Miriam held her lids tighter.

"No," he spoke evenly. "We've come to stop you."

"We are praising and preparing." He let out a long laugh.

"You are-"

"What is this thing you have done?" Moses'

unmistakable voice cracked the air around Miriam.

Without thought, she opened her eyes wide and searched for his face.

He stood behind Aaron with tablets of stone in both hands. She could see writing on the backside of them.

"Brother." Aaron rose a cup. The movement caused its contents to spill out. "Good of you to join us too."

A group of men laughed.

Miriam noticed Joshua's wide gaze. He was just over Moses' right shoulder as he took in the scene as well.

Moses threw the stone tablets at Aaron's feet.

The laughter ceased.

Miriam watched Moses' attention turn to the golden calf. He glanced back to his brother and, for a moment, his eyes fell on her before he stomped over to the image and picked it up.

"Brother, don't!"

Moses made his way over to a blazing fire that had been set for people to dance around. He tossed the calf in. His intense gaze fell over every face around him.

Miriam pushed in tighter against Caleb's back, hoping to hide from his fury. She peered around as people hurried to cover themselves. Some scattered.

"No one move," Moses ordered.

People halted their steps.

Miriam gulped for fresh air. Her heart pounded so loud she could feel it in her ears. Another small step forward brought her within a breath of Caleb's outer cloak. She wanted to reach out and pull it around herself.

When the fire smoldered to nothing, Moses collected the burned pieces of gold and ground them to powder.

Everyone watched his movements in silence.

"Follow me." He turned his back on the group.

People walked in complete silence behind him.

Miriam remained flanked behind Caleb as he moved. She knew she couldn't stay forever hiding in his shadow, but she was going to prolong being the focus of her brother's attention for as long as possible.

Moses took the powder down to the stream and tossed it over the water.

"Drink," he ordered.

Each person took their turn drinking a handful of the dirty water.

Miriam peered around Caleb to Eliora dipping her hand in the stream. Her heart gave a tight squeeze as she watched the midwife skim a handful of water into her palm. She sipped the water and swallowed hard. Miriam gagged at the thought of drinking the metallic water.

Her attention caught her brother staring at them. His gaze was hard and displeased.

"The members of our tribe did not participate in this foolishness." Caleb straightened himself under Moses' questioning eye.

"Very well. The tribe of Levi is excused from drinking."

Miriam sighed with relief.

Moses turned to face the others. "The Lord's anger is burning against you stiff-necked people. He informed me that you were down here worshiping an idol." His gaze washed over all of them as the last people came to get their drink from the stream. "I pleaded for Him to remember the promises He made with our fathers. I reminded Him that all Egypt would hear if He destroyed us."

Miriam's heart fluttered with fear.

"I reminded Him that if all this happened, then the world would disregard His power."

Her knees trembled.

"And so, He repented from His plan to wipe us from the earth."

She wanted to sigh with relief, but the fear was still too intense.

Moses turned to Aaron. "What did this people do to you to bring this great sin upon them?"

"Don't let your anger burn against me," Aaron pleaded, throwing himself at his brother's feet.

"You know these people. They are set on mischief."

Moses eyed the group before looking back down on his brother.

"They asked me to make them gods to go before us as we return to Egypt," Aaron's words fell out of his mouth in a quick-paced tumble. "You were gone so long that we didn't know what had happened to you." He pulled the hem of Moses' tunic. "I asked them to bring any gold to me and they did. After I collected it, I threw it all into the fire and the calf leapt out of the flames."

Miriam's heart skipped a beat. She didn't understand why Aaron was lying, but she wasn't brave enough to correct him. Her knees trembled again.

Moses looked over the people who stood silent as Aaron revealed their sin.

She followed his gaze.

Many had their heads bowed and huddled together.

"Who is on the Lord's side?" Moses inquired. "Let them come unto me."

Caleb took a few steps toward him.

Miriam wanted to cling to his cloak, but she held her place.

The other men from her tribe joined Caleb's side and the women soon followed.

She made her way to stand beside Elisheba.

"This is what the Lord, God of Israel, has said, 'Put every man his sword by his side and go in and out from gate to gate through the camp. Slay every man his brother, and every man his companion, and every man his neighbor.' " Moses instructed.

Miriam's breath caught in her parched throat.

"Consecrate yourselves to the Lord," he ordered.

The men of Levi obeyed without question and went to fetch their swords from the tent.

Miriam reached for Elisheba who clung to her.

"What are we going to do?" The woman's frightened eyes pleaded with Miriam.

"We are going to return to Eleazar's tent and wait for this to pass." She gathered the women and herded them away.

She caught Caleb's glance as she pushed the last Levite woman into the tent.

He stepped closer to her.

She saw the glint of the sword in his hand. "I'll keep the women safe in here."

He nodded. "Stay the night." With a dash, he left her.

Miriam tucked past the flap. She found the women huddled together around the open space.

Elisheba reached up for her.

She knelt beside her sister-in-law.

"What is going to happen?"

"I'm not certain." She chewed her bottom lip.

"Moses was so angry."

"The Lord is angry."

Miriam couldn't argue.

The night held screams of agony outside the walls of the goat-skinned tent.

Many of the women trembled in their sleep around her. Miriam dared not close her eyes. She feared if she did that her own image would display a close replica of the horror that was happening outside her vision.

It was somewhere in the deepest dark of night that her eyelids fell too heavy to fight. She dreamed of people dancing naked around the shining calf and the scorching gaze of her brother. She wanted to run to him and explain, but she couldn't reach him.

The next morning, she woke to the quiet sounds of women waiting for word to leave the tent.

She stirred. "Wait here. I'll see if it's safe."

Carefully, she peeled back the flap and stepped into the cool sand. The camp was quiet. She glanced around to find Caleb. He sat outside his nearby tent.

Miriam watched blood drip from the end of his sword. She knelt beside him.

His attention lifted to her. His face was hard and worn.

"Is it safe?" she asked softly. "For the women?"

He nodded.

She glared at the weapon again.

He followed her gaze.

"How many?"

"Three thousand men." He took the rag in his other hand and wiped the blade.

She rose slowly.

"Moses wants us to gather again," he spoke the words steadily. "He has more to say."

She nodded and returned to the tent.

"Has the judgment passed?" Elisheba asked.

She nodded slowly. "We are to gather to hear from Moses."

Her sister-in-law stood. "Then we shall gather at once."

Miriam walked with the women, but her thoughts were on the bloody sword in Caleb's hand. It dripped with the life force of those who had sinned. Though none of her tribe's blood was found on a sword from the previous night, the men who were slaughtered in the night were still her people.

How many more widows will I have to see in the coming days?

Three thousand men. Caleb's words haunted her.

Three thousand mothers, sisters, or wives to help prepare for life without their men.

Her shoulders buckled under the weight laid

upon her heart.

"You have sinned a great sin," Moses' words were as heavy as the load she felt. "Now, I will go up unto the Lord so I can make an atonement for your sin."

Miriam watched him disappear into the clouds. She prayed silently that he would return before the setting of the sun. She feared what the people would do if he were gone for another extended stay.

She sat at the foot of the mountain waiting, but it was thankfully only a few hours when Moses returned.

He met her with a furious look on his face. Dread and anger mixed with weariness. She hated seeing him carry such a burden alone.

"What does God say?" she asked.

"He has accepted the atonement, but payment must still be made."

Without further explanation, Moses turned away.

Miriam looked up to the shadowy cloud. Flashes lit up the darkness. Her heart beat wildly. Many men were already slain for the sin. What else did God have planned for the people?

Late into the night, she lay on her mat on the women's side of her family's tent. She tried to sleep, but her mind would not cease with everything that had happened. Dreams woke her frequently. The tent around her shook with a violent wind. It frightened her more than the dreams that invaded her mind.

She had endured a fair amount of stormy nights sleeping out in the wilderness. This was unlike any storm so far. An eerie presence hung in the air. She felt as if some form floated through the tents. Not a welcomed one like the pillar of cloud and fire. This form brought fear. Fear of what she would discover come first light. Faces of widows danced in her mind. She ached for them.

When the rays of early sun roused her, she sat up. She held her breath, not knowing what she was waiting to hear or see. Everything was still. Too still. The wind that blew all night was now still. The presence was gone, but emptiness had taken its place.

She quickly changed dresses and held the curtain in her grasp. She dared a peek into the open area, but no one was there. With haste, she rushed to Eliora's tent. She had not seen her friend since early the previous morning.

When she got to the midwife's tent, she glanced in to see Eliora's form lying on her mat. It was unlike her to still be asleep at this time of the morning. She lightly stepped over to her and placed a hand on the woman's shoulder. She gently tried to rouse her friend.

As Eliora turned over, Miriam held her hands

to her mouth in a gasp. The midwife's once beautiful olive complexion was now yellow-green with illness. Miriam could see open sores on her neck.

"Eliora!' She gasped again. "What has happened to you?"

"Miriam?" her voice broke as if parched.

She reached up to grab Eliora's water skin and lifted it to her friend's mouth. "Drink."

She obeyed.

Miriam noticed her crusted eyes. She rushed over to grab a rag from a medical bag and then turned the water skin over onto it to wet it. She tenderly wiped her friend's eyes.

"What's wrong?" Eliora whispered.

"You're ill."

Shock lit up her face.

"I don't know what's going on." She wiped her friend's eyes clean again.

Eliora blinked a few times and then lifted her arms to her face. "Sores?"

"They are on your neck as well."

She slowly lowered her arms back to her sides and closed her eyes.

"Tell me what to do," Miriam pleaded.

"I have some salve in my bag. Bring it with some fresh bandages."

She rushed to obey. With Eliora's instructions, she carefully cleaned and applied salve to the open wounds and bound them neatly.

"You're so pale."

"I don't feel well." Eliora groaned.

"Rest," she ordered. "I'm going to find help."

In the next tent over Miriam searched for Jola, another midwife.

She found her bent over her daughter.

"Jola, please come help. It's Eliora."

The midwife turned toward her.

Miriam saw the young girl lying very still. Jola was wrapping fresh bandages on her arm.

"Oh no," she gasped. "Her too?"

She tilted her head to the side. "Too?"

"It's Eliora. She looks like that." She motioned to the girl.

Jola dipped her head.

Miriam noticed a bandage across her neck. "You as well?"

She nodded. "I'll be over at once."

Miriam hurried back to Eliora's tent. "Jola is coming. Hold on."

As if called, Jola appeared by their side. "She looks worse than Geela."

"She's sick as well?" Eliora groaned.

Miriam and Jola exchanged a glance.

"I am too." The other midwife pushed up a sleeve to reveal another bandage. "The pain woke me before dawn. I checked on my daughter and she was the same."

"What's going on?" Eliora questioned.

"I don't know." Jola shook her head. "It's not like anything I've seen before."

"Can you sit with them while I go find my brothers?" Miriam asked.

"Send any help you can find along the way."

"Of course." She turned to Eliora. "I'll be back to check on you soon."

Eliora nodded slowly. She winced at the pain the movement caused.

Miriam hurried through the encampment. She found Moses and Aaron in the tent they had set up to receive people.

"Moses." Miriam pushed her way through the group of people to find her brothers.

His attention fell to her. "Miriam? Why are you out of breath?"

"It's Eliora and Jola and Geela," she huffed. "They are all sick."

"Take a look around," Moses said, looking over her head.

Miriam turned to glance at the people she had moved past. Many of them had bandages covering their skin or held onto those too sick to walk.

"What is going on?" she asked.

"A plague," Aaron replied.

She turned back to her brothers.

"God's punishment for sin," Moses clarified.

"What are we to do?" She held her cheeks.

"Whatever we can to help them," Aaron answered.

"I'll go through the midwives and see who is not ill. They will help."

Moses nodded.

Miriam set to work checking on each midwife she could find. It seemed the plague hit almost every tent. Every tent except the tribe of Levi. They were unaffected by the illness.

She gathered her family members and set each to work. She borrowed supplies from the midwives and saw to as many as she could late into the evening. It wasn't until she ran out of supplies that she finally stopped. She came near to Eliora's tent once again. She had sent Elisheba to check on her a few hours prior, but she wanted to see her friend.

"How are you feeling?" she asked, kneeling beside her.

"Your sister-in-law brought me some fresh manna cakes." She pointed to the small wrapped bundle.

"Have you been able to eat?"

Eliora frowned.

Miriam picked up the bundle and lifted the top cake. She held it out to Eliora's mouth. "Here."

Eliora's lips closed around the cake and she bit off a small bite. She chewed slowly. When she cleared her mouth, she asked, "Any word?"

Miriam lifted the cake to her lips again for a second bite. "It seems most of the camp has the same illness." She shook her head.

"Anzety? And the other midwives?"

"Them as well." She offered another bite. "My family has spread as far as we could help." She fought the urge to cry. "Your guild offered their supplies, but they are just as ill. Some offered to help, but I could see how weak they were simply tying their own bandages."

Eliora took another bite and then waved off the rest.

Miriam refolded the bundle. "I don't know what to do," she whispered. "I'm afraid we don't have enough to help everyone."

Eliora patted her arm with her bandaged hand.

"Moses says this is from God." She trembled. "A punishment."

"Then we will accept his will."

Miriam gazed down at her ill friend. She looked as pale as Puah had the last night she saw her alive. Her heart gave a tight squeeze. She couldn't bear the thought of losing Eliora too.

"Hold on, my friend. Hold on." She laid her head beside Eliora's bandaged arm and wept. Her silent prayers lifted as far as she could stretch them to the One who was always near enough to hear.

Chapter 12

*"And the LORD spake unto Moses face to face,
as a man speaketh unto his friend."*
-EXODUS 33:11

Miriam watched the cloud-covered mountain.

"It's been forty days," Aaron's voice was low beside her.

She turned her face just enough to glare at him through sideways eyes. "And we will wait as long as it takes for him to return." She set her gaze back to the mountain.

In the stirring cover, a form appeared and then a second.

Miriam held her breath.

A few moments passed before she could see Moses climbing down with Joshua close behind.

"Thanks be to God," Aaron replied.

She bounced from one foot to another, waiting on the safe side of the border to embrace her brother.

As he came close to the bottom, she saw the

stone tablets in his hand that he had carved himself. The first two had been made and written on by God. These were carved by Moses and had similar writing on them.

As he closed the last few feet between them, Miriam thought she saw a flash of lightning near him. She reached for him instinctively to protect her younger brother.

Aaron grabbed her arm and pulled her back.

She turned to see him shielding his eyes from the light.

Gasps came from behind them as Aaron continued to drag her backward.

Miriam tried to face the bright light, but she could only squint in its direction.

"Brother," she called out.

"I am he," Moses answered.

She could feel Aaron's hand quiver around hers, but he didn't release her.

"Here," she heard Joshua's voice.

When the brightness dulled, Miriam was able to look on her brother.

Joshua had given up his headwrap to cover Moses' face like a veil.

Rays of light still shone under the cover, but at least they could look in his direction without being blinded.

"Come," Moses encouraged with outstretched arms.

Miriam took a step, but Aaron still held her arm. She turned and patted his hand. "It's well, brother."

He slowly lifted each finger in turn.

She turned to see Moses again. "I'm so glad you returned."

He nodded. "I have word from the Lord."

"Then we shall hear it," Aaron replied.

The people were called and gathered to hear the latest message.

"Take from among you," Moses said in a voice that carried not only volume but authority. "An offering unto the Lord. Whoever is of a willing heart, let him bring an offering of gold, silver, brass, blue, purple, scarlet, fine linen, goat's hair, badgers' skins, shittim wood, oil, spices, sweet incense, onyx stones, and others. We will take all the offerings and construct a tabernacle with furniture."

Miriam moved with the flow of people back to the tents. She rummaged through her belongings to find items she had brought from Egypt. She collected a pile in her sack and return to the field at the foot of the mountain.

Moses had stationed men to help collect the contributions.

Miriam walked up to Joshua and handed over her pouch filled with precious stones and golden bracelets.

He smiled at her as he accepted the offering.

"What was it like up there?" she whispered.

"Remind me to tell you about it some time." He glanced up at the mount with longing.

She nodded and stepped aside to allow the next person in line to give him their bag.

"The Lord has called Bezaleel, son of Uri, grandson of Hur of the tribe of Judah," Moses called.

Bezaleel stepped forward.

Miriam saw Hur's face beam with pride.

"The Lord has filled him with His Spirit in wisdom, and understanding, and knowledge in all manner of workmanship," Moses continued. "He has also put in his heart to teach. He will teach Aholiab, son of Ahisamach, of the tribe of Dan." He paused and waited for the man to step forward and take his place beside Bezaleel. "He has filled them with wisdom of heart in order to do the work of engraving for the tabernacle."

Cheers rose from the crowd.

Miriam met Joshua on the way to the meeting tent where Moses had instructed Bezaleel to filter through the collections.

"So?" she encouraged. "What was it like?"

He matched her excited pace. "I didn't get to go as close as Moses, but I could sense the presence of the Lord. I heard thunders which Moses said was the Lord speaking."

"You didn't hear for yourself?"

"The words weren't meant for me." He shrugged. "When they are, I'll hear them."

"When?"

He nodded and adjusted the load on his back. "Moses told me the Lord wants him to train me as his replacement."

"In Canaan?"

His eyes glistened. "I can't wait."

"Are you coming to the wedding feast next week?"

"I've been invited by Moses."

"Good. I know Bezaleel will be happy to have you."

Miriam slipped her finest dress over her head and set it neatly on her body. She took extra time preparing her hair as well.

The construction on the tabernacle was going smoothly as the men worked day and night carving. But tonight was a celebration. Bezaleel's daughter, Eliraz, was to be married to Amir. The parents of both had matched them soon after their birth and the time was right for them to join together.

Miriam came upon the open gathering.

Everyone was dressed in their best. The women of both families had taken great care to decorate the space with the most beautiful drapings. Desert flowers hung from every tent pole. Their delicate fragrances enveloped Miriam as she came closer. It looked like an oasis.

The bridegroom, Amir, and his collection of men entered the area with an ornamentally decorated Eliraz.

Miriam glanced at Bezaleel and his family. They all beamed so proudly.

She returned her gaze to the approaching group as Amir led the way. They came toward the center of the gathering, where Moses stood waiting for them.

"We gather as a people to bless this happy couple," Moses said. His voice was light and filled with joy. "God of the universe, we bless Your name. We thank You for all Your many blessings and we ask a special blessing on this couple as they join as one. Leaving their families and cleaving to each other as You called all to do from the time of Adam and Eve. Expand their tent and bring them a long life of obedience to Your word."

The couple pressed close for their first kiss as the crowd shouted.

"And now the couple will retire to their prepared bedchamber," Moses proclaimed.

Miriam caught the blush on Eliraz's cheeks

under her thin veil as her bridegroom led her away.

It had been a week since Moses had come down from the mountain. The shine from his time with God had worn from his face to the point that a veil was no longer required. She smiled at his warm glance.

Miriam found Eliraz's mother, Inbar, serving her guests. "She's a beautiful bride," she greeted the happy mother.

"She is, isn't she." Inbar clasped her hands together. "I'm so happy you could join us today to celebrate."

"I am as well." She picked up a manna cake. "I hear your husband has been working hard on the furniture for the tabernacle."

She nodded. "He's rarely taken a break."

"I supposed that's why God has repeatedly stressed to us about not taking the Sabbath for granted. Otherwise, we shall all work ourselves to an early death."

"That is certainly true for my husband. Sleep even gets in his way," she joked.

"God chose a good man."

"That he did." Her smile widened.

Miriam danced with the other women and chatted between songs.

Finally, the couple emerged from the chamber with evidence of their union.

When the cheering died down, Bezaleel spoke, "Daughter, will you please come here." He waved her over to a table where a large object sat covered. "Your mother and I have a gift to present to you."

He patted the hidden object. "Daughter, we wish you love, happiness, and prosperity all the days of your life. Out of our love, we have made this gift for you," Bezaleel said as he lifted the blanket.

Gasps filled the large tent as the guests stared at the beautifully crafted wooden box. The large chest shone with a dark polish Bezaleel had added to bring out the small details of the wood. Freshly chopped cedar from the hills in Lebanon could not be mistaken for anything else. The aroma was so sweetly intoxicating Miriam had to resist the urge to edge closer for a better smell. The gift was magnificent and, all the more so, because it came from the hands of the father of the bride.

"For me?" Eliraz whispered.

"For you, my daughter."

"Father, it's so wonderful." She embraced him. "Thank you."

"Thank you, my daughter. This gift comes from my love for you. Cherish it, as I have cherished you." He cupped her face in his hands and kissed her forehead.

"Father...it's just so beautiful," she said as she gently ran her fingers over the smooth, polished wood.

"Bezaleel," Amir called, as he made his way to his new father-in-law's side. "You have made your daughter truly happy. Thank you for such a gift."

"This gift, I hope, will bring her much joy. In turn, I hope she brings you as much joy as she has brought to my family." He looked back at his daughter. "Open it up, my dear. Your mother has filled it with much for you."

Eliraz looked in on the wonderful new garments her mother had made for her and breathed in the sweet smell of cedar. She closed the lid gently and looked over at her mother, who was sobbing uncontrollably in the arms of her oldest son.

She pulled her mother close to her chest and stroked her head. "There, there, Mother. Everything will be alright."

"I'm just so happy, child."

"I am too."

Miriam couldn't suppress the smile that spread across her face. This was how life was supposed to be. Parents passing down to their children. Love filling all and spreading out to fill the room. Friends and family enjoying life together. Joy, hope, and love merging together in a contagious outstretching that touched every person present. This was freedom. This was a promise fulfilled from the Garden of Eden.

Chapter 13

"According to all that the LORD commanded Moses, so the children of Israel made all the work."
-EXODUS 39:42

Two hundred and five days after Moses laid out the plan for the tabernacle the time had finally arrived to assemble all of the pieces. It was the first day of the first month of the second year since they had left Egypt. Hope started to slip through Miriam's fingers that they would reach the promised land in time for any of them to enjoy it.

Every member of the tribe of Levi was gathered and ready to help Moses assemble the tabernacle for the first time. She stood with the women to witness the event unfold.

Bezaleel brought forward his masterpiece. The ark of the covenant was larger than the hope chest he had constructed for his daughter, but it showed similar design.

Miriam admired how the gold caught the

sunlight. It shone as bright as Moses' face when he came down the last time from the mountain.

The chest was two and a half cubits long, a cubit and a half wide and just as tall. He had overlaid the shittim wood with pure gold. Around the top of it was a crown of gold as well.

On each of the corners were rings of gold. The staves which bore the weight where also shittim wood overlaid with gold. He and his apprentice, Aholiab, were at the two front corners carrying the ark forward. Two others helped carry the staves on their shoulders.

On top of the main box sat a seat of gold. It held two carved figures. Cherubim made of gold, beaten out of one piece seated at the two ends of the lid. Their wings were spread wide and high covering the seat. They faced each other and toward the center of the lid.

Miriam felt a tingle run through her skin as the ark passed by her. It was warm and comforting. Like the presence that had whispered to her on countless occasions.

She wondered how Bezaleel had managed to depict the angels' faces. No one had seen one except for the man that told them to follow the cloud pillar. She noticed they shared some of his features.

Moses directed the men toward the area next to him. The four men laid the box down carefully on the prepared spot and removed the staves.

Aaron and several other men helped Moses lift the walls of the tent around the ark to act as a veil that would block it from outside view.

The curtains were a gorgeous mix of reds and blues sewn by expert hands. Miriam watched it fall perfectly into place, sweeping the sand to completely incase the ark behind its cover.

She stepped back as Moses moved further away from the curtain.

He motioned Bezaleel forward with the next piece. A table that was two cubits long, a cubit wide, and a cubit and a half high. It was made just like the ark. Shittim wood covered by pure gold and topped with a crown. At its four corners were also rings of gold inserted with gold staves for carrying.

The men placed the table where Moses pointed and left to bring in the next piece.

Moses reached out toward Miriam. She stepped forward with the sack in her hand.

One by one, Moses removed the contents. Dishes, spoons, bowls, and cups all made from pure gold. Moses laid each one on the table in the order that God had instructed him. When he was finished, he nodded in approval.

Miriam stepped to the side with the empty sack in her hands. She twisted it, wishing to be of more help.

Next came the lampstand. Moses motioned for Bezaleel to place it on the opposite side of the area from the table. It had six branches stemming from its center shaft having three on each side. Each branch was covered in flowers and the top held a bowl for oil.

He carefully added the oil to bowls and then lit them.

Bezaleel returned with another large piece. An altar for incense was a cubit long and wide. It was two cubits high and the horns were another two cubits high coming out from the corners. A crown of gold also rounded its top to match the ark and table. There were two rings under the crown for the staves which helped the carriers bear it. Moses instructed him to place it in front of the veil, which hid the ark.

When he returned to the tent, Bezaleel handed Moses containers of oil, spices, and incense.

After double checking all the pieces, Moses nodded for everyone to back away. He motioned for the outer curtains to be set in place.

The tent was constructed from the inside out and Miriam stopped with the group who witnessed its first construction.

A large laver was brought next. It was made of polished brass collected from the women.

Miriam looked at the women who were gathered behind her. Their faces were bright and joyful at the laver being put into place.

An altar was the final piece brought into place in front of the laver. It was five cubits long and wide and three cubits high. It had matching horns to the incense altar inside the tent except these were brass where the others were gold. All of its accompanying accessories were also made of brass. Its four corners held rings for carrying as well.

Moses stepped even further back from the pieces.

The people responded with backward steps.

Men lifted the court posts into place around the tabernacle and laver and altar. They attached the curtains which would designate the holy space from the rest of the camp. People huddled around the open gate staring into the courtyard where Moses stood alone.

He held a bowl of anointing oil in his hand and moved about the different spaces anointing everything. When he came back into the courtyard from the inner tent, the cloud moved from the mountain and rested over the covered center tent where the ark was placed.

He stepped to the curtain again and tried to enter, but he could not. He turned to gaze at Miriam.

She shrugged.

He tried again, but was unable to move forward.

Miriam watched him hesitate. She wasn't sure what to do as she stood there holding her breath with the rest of the congregation.

Moses turned to face Aaron. He stepped closer to his brother and put a hand on his shoulder. "Bring the tribe of Levi to the door and we shall prepare them for service."

Aaron headed into the crowd to gather his sons.

"What is it, brother?" Miriam asked Moses.

"Because of the sin of the people, we can't enter unclean." He looked up to the cloud. "The Levites will be our mediators between the people and God and our representation from God to the people."

"All Levites?" Her heart skipped a beat.

Moses didn't answer as Aaron returned with his four sons.

Miriam smiled like a proud mother at Nadab, Abihu, Eleazar, and Ithamar. They stood tall behind their father.

The rest of Miriam's tribe clustered behind them waiting to hear from Moses. She moved to stand with them.

"These are the things which the Lord has commanded to be done," Moses voice rang out over the gathering. " 'Count the sons of Levi from one-month-old upward.' "

Miriam stood in the midst of her tribe.

Moses passed by each member, counting the males.

When he came to the end, he shouted, "Twenty-two thousand is the number of Levities. Now those who are the family of Kohath from thirty years old until fifty shall be separated for service. These men shall be those who will carry the most holy things.

"When it is time for camp to go out, Aaron and his sons will take down the veil and cover the ark with it. They shall also lay over it a covering of badger's skin and a blue cloth. Over the table, they will place a blue cloth, a scarlet cloth, and a badger's skin. Covering of blue and badger's skin shall also cover the candlestick, incense altar and all the instruments of ministry. The ashes of the altar shall be separated and covered with a purple cloth.

"When everything is covered, the sons of Kohath will come forward to bear it as we march. When the cloud pillar stops and we assemble the tabernacle, the sons of Kohath shall not touch any holy thing lest they die. They may only touch the item once it is covered."

He glanced over at Aaron's sons. "Aaron and his sons will go in and appoint every one of them an item and that will be their burden to carry every time we move.

"Count the sons of Gershon for they will also

serve to do the work of the tabernacle of the congregation," Moses continued. "They shall bear the curtains and the coverings which will also be appointed by Aaron and his sons.

"As for the sons of Merari, they will be assigned the boards, bars, pillars, and sockets of the courtyard."

The tribe of Levi returned to the congregation.

"Moses," Miriam whispered as she stepped closer. "Do those past the age of fifty have no way to serve?"

"This is what the Lord has commanded," he stated simply. "It is not my place to question what he has said."

"But those of us who have strength enough to serve-"

He held up his palm to her. "This is what the Lord has commanded."

She bit her bottom lip and took a step back.

"Now bring forth Aaron and his sons," Moses requested.

When Aaron and his four sons came forward, Moses took each man and prepared his body with water. Upon Aaron, he placed a set of new garments Blue, purple, and scarlet covered each man. Moses lifted an ephod of gold, blue, purple, and scarlet and fine twined linen over Aaron's head to lay it against his chest. The polished stones shone well in the light and reflected their individual colors. Each stone was engraved with one of the names of the twelve children of Israel.

A bright red sardius etched with Reuben's name was the first that caught her eye. It was followed by a yellowish-brown topaz engraved with Simeon and an emerald carbuncle with Levi inscribed on it completed the top row.

The second row continued the birth order of the twelve sons of Israel. A bright green emerald for Judah, a brilliant blue sapphire for Dan, and a clear diamond for Naftali.

The third row was filled with an amber ligure for Gad, a brown layered agate for Asher, and a purple amethyst for Issachar.

And the last row contained a yellowish beryl for Zebulun, an onyx with a mix of black, white, and red for Joseph, and a rich red jasper for Benjamin.

Each stone was set in gold which enclosed them into the breastplate.

From the bottom of the breastplate hung chains of pure gold that made clinking sounds when Aaron moved. Blue lace girded the ephod around him and a carefully-woven blue robe was added. On the hems of the robe were bells of gold alternated with pomegranates. Moses placed the shoulder pads on top of the ephod. Each shoulder also bore the names of the tribes.

On Aaron's head, Moses placed a mitre with a gold band across the front. An inscription across the front read, "Holiness to the Lord."

Into the breastplate, Moses slipped the Urim and the Thummim. These would be used to discern the will of the Lord.

He took similar garments and placed them on Aaron's sons.

When he was done dressing the men, Moses nodded to a man standing by. He led a young bull forward. Aaron and his sons laid their hands upon the animal's head for a sin offering.

Moses took his sharpened knife and slit the animal's throat. He collected the free-flowing blood in a small bowl. He wiped some of the blood on the horns of the altar and the rest of the animal was burned.

Moses motioned for another man to step forward with a ram. In the same manner, Aaron and his sons laid their hands on the ram's head. Moses killed it and collected blood to sprinkle on the altar.

With a second ram, after Aaron and his sons laid hands on the animal, Moses took its blood and marked Arron's right ear, right thumb, and large toe of his right foot. He repeated the process with each of Aaron's sons.

As Miriam watched the wave offering and all the pieces of meat pass from hand to hand, her mouth watered. The smell of burning flesh made her stomach grumble. Even the fresh loaves of bread added their sweet savor to the smells filling her nose.

Moses took some of the blood and sprinkled Aaron's garments and his sons'.

"Boil the flesh at the door of the tabernacle and eat it with the bread," he told his brother.

Aaron led his sons to the door of the tabernacle to obey.

Miriam watched them carefully as the meat cooked.

When it was done, Aaron retrieved it from the water and gave some to each of his sons with the bread from the wave offering.

Miriam grabbed her midsection. It had been a while since she ate meat. The satisfying taste of roasted quail stirred up her mouth to water again. With each bite she watched them eat, her mouth opened as if waiting for them to throw her a piece.

When they had their fill, they passed the leftovers to Moses.

He walked past Miriam and the others who witnessed the event. She almost reached for the plate but held her arms by her side.

Where is he taking the rest?

She watched as he headed in the same direction he had taken parts of the bull.

No.

Within moments, a thin pillar of smoke came from the same place in the distance as it had before.

Moses returned with the empty plate. Some of the juices of the meat still shined in the sunlight on the platter.

Miriam wanted to lick the delicious juices. She could almost taste them on her tongue.

"For the next seven days you will not leave the courtyard of the tabernacle," Moses said toward the group of newly anointed priests. "Each day you will consecrate yourselves until the week is done."

A week? They get to eat like that for a week?

Her empty stomach protested. She wondered if she could resist the urge to scramble for the scraps before the fire licked them up for an entire week.

Chapter 14

"And Nadab and Abihu, the sons of Aaron, took either of them his censer, and put fire therein, and put incense thereon, and offered strange fire before the LORD, which he commanded them not."
-LEVITICUS 10:1

For seven days, Miriam stood outside the tabernacle watching Aaron and his sons repeat the long anointing process over and over again.

Her stomach turned over on manna cakes every time she saw them eating the boiled meat and fresh flatbread.

She restrained as she watched Moses take their leftovers and burned them outside the camp for seven days straight.

"Why can't we eat it?" she asked her brother on the seventh night.

He simply stared at her as if she'd grown an extra limb.

"Why does it have to be burned?" she

continued. "We barely have any food."

"The Lord has provided manna for us every morning," he argued. "He provides clean drinking water for us every time we ask." He shook his head. "How can you ask for what has been separated for Himself?"

"I just don't understand why the surplus has to be destroyed. Why not give it out?"

"The Lord has separated the food for His separated."

"I just don't-"

He held up his hand. "The matter is settled."

She stood and huffed behind the divider curtain. Kneeling on her mat, she crossed her legs and held her chin in her hands. "It's not right to burn up all that meat."

She laid down and tossed to fight the warring urges within. Finally, she settled into a light sleep.

Moses called the elders to the tabernacle the following morning.

Miriam trailed him wanting to know what would happen since the week of separation was done for the new priests.

"Aaron," Moses called. "Take these." He led three young calves and a ram into the tabernacle.

"Offer them before the Lord."

He turned to the people gathered and said, "Take a young goat for a sin offering, and a calf and a lamb both in their first year without blemish for a burnt offering. Also, take a young bull and a ram for peace offerings. All of these are to be mingled with oil and then sacrificed to the Lord because today the Lord will appear before you."

People disappeared into the fields where the animals were kept and returned with the ones Moses had requested.

Aaron and his sons killed, collected, and sorted all the pieces of offerings.

Moses and Aaron were able to enter the tabernacle together and were not held back by the Lord. When they returned, they blessed the people. Fire came down and consumed all the had been placed on the altar.

Miriam saw the pillar of fire lap up the offering and she fell on her face.

Many of those around her did the same.

As the pillar calmed, the people rose and went about their day.

Miriam's days consisted of trips from one widow's tent to another. She met Eliora on the path between the tents one evening.

"You look spent," her friend commented.

Miriam sighed. "I feel old."

"I don't think it's just your age."

She tilted her head.

"You are carrying as heavy a burden as your brother tried when he sat on his judgment seat listening to the people's arguments."

Miriam remembered her brother's worn face each night.

"Didn't your father-in-law give him counsel?"

She nodded. "Jethro told him to spread the load over many shoulders."

"Maybe you should take the same advice."

'You know," she thought about the idea. "I have been meaning to discuss that very thing with you."

"Me?"

"I was hoping your guild could help look after the widows."

"Many of us would be happy to help."

"I know some of those with illnesses would benefit from your knowledge."

"I'll meet you in your tent in the morning and you can show me around to those who need us."

She smiled, but it faded. "There have just been so many widows recently."

Eliora placed her hand on Miriam's shoulder. "We will make sure they are under our wings."

She embraced her.

Miriam left her friend with a grateful heart and a lightened step. She headed back to her tent, but paused at the gate of the tabernacle to watch

Aaron, Eleazar, and Ithamar hard at work. She longed to join them. She wanted to be of use.

Her gaze skimmed the courtyard. "Aaron," she called.

He stepped closer to her.

"Where are your other sons?"

Aaron glanced around. "They were here a moment ago." He took a second look around.

A pillar of fire abruptly came down in the midst of the inner tent.

Aaron looked to his two sons.

Eleazer's eyes were stuck on the pillar.

Ithamar covered his face.

Moses rushed into the courtyard directly to Aaron. "What has happened?" he asked. "I saw the pillar."

"We didn't place any sacrifices in there," Aaron answered.

Moses looked around the area. "Where are Nadab and Abihu?"

"I don't know," he answered.

Moses walked into the inner tent and returned within a moment.

Miriam stood in horror at the grim look on his face. His skin was pale and his eyes burned with hatred.

"What have they done?" he accused Aaron.

He shook his head and stepped toward the tent.

Moses held him back. "They have offered strange fire before the Lord."

Aaron opened his mouth to speak, but then held his peace and looked to the sand.

"Mishael and Elzaphan," Moses called to their cousins.

The men ran toward him.

"Go in and carry your family out. Take them outside the camp."

They bowed and went into the tent to obey.

Each man carried one of the bodies out and had wrapped their coats around them to cover their faces.

Moses walked over to Eleazer and Ithamar. "Don't uncover your heads." He glanced at Aaron. "Don't tear your clothes or you will die." His glance landed on Miriam. "But let your family and the whole house of Israel lament the burning which the Lord has kindled."

"Should we remove their priestly garments?" Eleazar asked as he watched the men walk by.

Moses looked at Mishael and Elzaphan, who had paused at the door. "No."

Miriam held her breath as the bodies passed.

One face came to her mind. She picked up the hem of her dress and ran as fast as she could back to her tent.

"Elisheba," she called, not waiting to make it into the tent. "Come quickly."

"What has gotten you so irritated?" Elisheba ducked her head out of the tent flap.

"It's Nadab and Abihu."

At the sound of her sons' names, she came closer to Miriam. She reached for her. "What has happened?"

"You must come." She laid a hand on her sister-in-law's arm and pulled. "You must come now."

The two ran together out of the camp.

When they found Mishael and Elzaphan, Miriam pointed to them. She tried to explain, but her throat tightened around the words.

Elisheba went up to her nephews and asked, "What has happened to my sons?"

The two exchanged a glance before facing their aunt.

"They offered strange fire before the Lord," Mishael answered.

"The Lord has dealt with them..." Elzaphan let his words trail off.

She glanced around them to the two covered bodies.

"No," she whispered. She fell beside them. "No!"

Miriam knelt beside her. She wrapped her arms around her as she rocked back and forth.

"No!" she wailed. "My sons!"

Miriam buried her face in her sister-in-law's

thick hair. Tears flowed from her eyes. She closed them and held on as tight as she could. She could hear shovels in the sand, but she kept her face hid.

"No, no, no…" Elisheba chanted. "Not my sons!"

When their nephews had finished their duty, they returned to the camp.

Miriam held Elisheba until she stopped rocking. They both stared at the two piles of sand until the sun hung low.

"Come," Miriam stood and led Elisheba back to their tent.

Each exchanged their dresses for ones of mourning.

The itchy sackcloth chafed Miriam's skin, but she resisted the urge to scratch. She wrapped a dark headcloth around her head and hugged her sister-in-law.

"There is something else I need to tell you," Miriam said.

Elisheba looked at her with fear in her eyes.

"Moses has ordered that Aaron and your other sons cannot mourn."

"What?" She squinted.

"He said they are separated now and need to continue with their duties. They can't defile themselves by mourning."

Elisheba shook her head and marched out of the tent.

Miriam noticed her direction was toward the tabernacle. She rose and followed without a word. She wanted to stop her, but didn't know what to say to even try.

They both halted at the door of the outer courtyard.

Moses stood in the middle of several of their family members.

She saw Elisheba open her mouth and then clamp it tightly shut. Her hands turned to fists beside her legs.

"You and your sons," Moses instructed Aaron and hesitated at the last word. "Take the meat offering that is left of the offerings of the Lord and eat it without leaven beside the altar because it is most holy. You will eat it in the holy place because it's your portion." He took a breath. "The breast from the wave offering and the shoulder from the heave offering you will eat in a clean place. You, your sons, and your daughters with you." He looked over to Miriam. "These are your portions which are given out of the sacrifices of peace offerings of the children of Israel. This is what the Lord has commanded."

Miriam would have smiled at the thought of being included into the Levities who would regularly feast on meat. It was a small joy when compared to the deaths of two of her nephews. She would trade every piece of shoulder to have them back.

As he turned to leave, Moses noticed pieces of a sin offering left on a table. "What is this?" he pointed to the sacrificed goat. "Why haven't you eaten the sin offering in the holy place? God has given it to you to bear the iniquity of the congregation in order to make atonement for them before the Lord."

He glanced around. "I see the bowl of blood, so it has not been taken into the holy place."

Aaron shook his head. "I was in such sorrow for what had befallen my family that I didn't know if it would be accepted by the Lord. So, we burned the meat since it was a goat and not a bull." A single tear ran down his cheek.

Moses pondered his words for a few moments and then laid a hand on his brother's shoulder. He nodded once and then left the courtyard.

As he passed, Elisheba held her tongue no longer. "How could you?" she accused.

He turned to face her.

"My sons…" her words faltered. "My husband…"

"Are serving the Lord," he finished her thought.

"Two of my sons are dead because of you."

Miriam prayed silently that Elisheba would find enough restraint not to spit on Moses. She stepped closer in case she needed to hold her back from attacking.

"Your sons are dead because they disobeyed the Lord," he explained. "They offered strange fire on the altar of incense when it was not-"

"They were serving there because you told them to," her voice rose in volume.

"They were there because the Lord had called them to serve," he said calmly.

"And now my husband and other sons can't even mourn them."

"They need to remain at their duty. They have an obligation to fulfill to the Lord."

"I'm starting to think that Zipporah was right about you," she flung the hate-filled words at him. "You are nothing but a self-centered old man who doesn't care about anyone else." She turned and ran away.

Moses hung his head.

Miriam reached over and squeezed his hand. "I'll speak to her."

Chapter 15

"And the wave breast and heave shoulder shall ye eat in a clean place; thou, and thy sons, and thy daughters with thee:"
-LEVITICUS 10:14

Miriam sat among family in one of her nephew's tents.

"Thank you for offering your area," Moses said to Eleazar.

"It's my pleasure." The younger man smiled and glanced around the crowded space. "Though I think it's about time to expand my tent again."

"It would seem so." Moses chuckled.

Aaron placed the platters of shoulder and breast meat in the center of the group. "I think you should offer the blessing, brother. We've prayed all day." He stifled a laugh.

Moses raised his arms. "Lord of the universe, we thank You for the meat You have provided. We thank You for answering our prayers and providing ways to live in peace with You and each other."

Miriam peeked over at Zipporah and Elisheba. They sat outside the circle busying themselves with some of their grandchildren.

"We bless You now as we receive from You."

Aaron and Moses took the first scoops and then the others joined in.

Miriam grabbed for a large piece of shoulder. She lifted it to her mouth and savored the delicate meat on her tongue. She chewed slowly, enjoying each moment of flavor.

The second piece she ate quicker and a third even faster. Her heart raced a little as the platter emptied.

When she tried to reach for one of the last remaining fragments, she caught Moses' stare. His icy glare went through her and she held her breath. Her glance landed on the floor and she pulled her arm back. She folded her hands in her lap and waited in silence until everyone was done.

Miriam helped the other women clear away the dirty dishes. She set to work just outside the tent flap with a bowl of water and a clean rag.

"We will need all the help we can get," she heard Moses' deep voice inside.

"Do you know how long that will take?" Eleazar asked.

"If we have help, it won't take as long as you think."

"To number the whole congregation?"

"That's what the Lord has requested. Everyone except the Levities."

"Why not us?" Ithamar's voice was defensive.

"The Lord has separated our family out of the whole to serve Him. This census will be for those who will be fighting for our promised land."

"Like an army?" Eleazar attempted.

"An army who will be used of the Lord to bring us into the land of Canaan," Moses clarified. "Our family will also lead the way when we head into the land."

"We are finally going into Canaan?" Ithamar's voice rose in excitement.

"Very soon."

There was quiet chatter for a few moments.

"Once we get all the tribes numbered we will also organize them around the tabernacle," Moses' voice broke through the excitement.

"This is starting to sound more and more like a battle plan," Eleazar added.

"And what of us?" Ithamar asked.

"We shall pitch our tents around the tabernacle. This will be a barrier for the people to protect them so no wrath will come upon them."

The next morning started early. Moses had repeated his instructions to the entire camp. Each family had taken the time to organize themselves into groups to be numbered.

The Levities and several other leaders went from group to group collecting the information and reporting back to Moses.

Miriam stood with the other Levite women near the front of the tabernacle.

Moses spent all morning scribbling on his parchments as each man brought him a tally.

When all the men over twenty had been counted, Joshua came near to Moses. "How many?" he asked.

He counted down his columns once and then a second time before answering, "Six hundred and three thousand five hundred and fifty men ready for battle."

Joshua looked out over his troops.

Miriam could tell he was pleased with the number.

"Now this is how we are to be arranged." Moses took a stick and drew in the sand.

She bent down to watch him draw.

"This is the tabernacle." He sketched a long rectangle. "Around it will be the Levities. On the south will be the family of Kohath, on the west will be the family of Gershon, the family of Meraribut will pitch on the north side and myself, Aaron and his sons will pitch in front of the door of the tabernacle to the east." He drew short squares around the rectangle as he spoke.

"To the East will be Judah, Issachar, and

Zebulun." He drew larger squares outside the small squares representing each tribe.

"To the South; Reuben, Simeon, and Gad. To the Wes; Ephraim, Mannasseh, and Benjamin." He continued his drawing all the way around. "And finally, to the North; Dan, Asher, and Naphatali."

Miriam admired the careful plan. It did remind her of the parchments of battle plans she had seen in Egypt.

For the next twelve days, the camp organized themselves as instructed. One tribe each day brought offerings to Aaron at the door of the tabernacle in the order assigned them by Moses.

Smoke filled the courtyard as each offering was presented. Aaron made sure they strictly followed every command they had been given.

Miriam spent days watching all the flesh be burned on the altar. Her stomach was filled each night with the shoulder and breast of those offerings.

On the twelfth night, she approached her brother before going to bed.

"I've wanted to ask a question," she said quietly.

"Ask on." Moses waved to her.

"You said the Levities would pitch their tents around the tabernacle."

He nodded.

"Those of Kohath's family to the south, but you and the priests will be at the door of the tabernacle."

He tilted his head for a moment, but then nodded again. "Myself, Aaron and his sons and their families."

"Exactly." She let out her breath. "I was thinking I could ask for my own tent in order to serve the women better."

"I don't understand."

"If I'm always here." She waved around the tent. "I don't always have an opportunity to welcome women in need."

"You can continue to visit their tents as you have done."

"I suppose." She wrung her hands. "But I think I could be of more use if I am in my own tent."

He rubbed his beard.

"Each of Jacob's wives had their own tent."

A smile pulled up the corners of his mouth. "I see you've thought about this a lot."

"Please, brother." She clasped her hands together in front of her.

"Do you have the material?"

"I've been saving goat's hair. I've almost got enough to make myself a small tent."

"Well." He reached to place a hand on her arm. "We shall make a place for your own tent."

"Thank you." She wrapped her arms around

his neck and hugged him tight.

Chapter 16

"*Your lamb shall be without blemish, a male of the first year...*"
-EXODUS 12:5

"Will you be joining us for the passover?" Moses asked Miriam as they walked toward the open fields.

"Of course," she replied. "I hadn't realized it was coming upon us so soon. My tent is not fully sewn yet. It will still be a few days before I can pitch it."

"Today is the tenth day of the first month. We need to pick out our lamb."

They came upon the shepherds tending the flocks.

"Kefir," Moses called.

The man waved from his knelt position in the middle of a group of yearlings.

Moses led Miriam through the herd.

Miriam noticed Kefir's dark hair curled slightly at the ends. It looked similar to the wool of the sheep he took care of. His beard was well kept and his eyes were lively. He rose to greet them.

"Are you well?" He patted a lamb who nudged his leg.

"I am," Moses answered. "How are our firstlings?"

"Strong as ever." His wide smile radiated with pride. "Would you like to see them?"

"That's why we've come."

The shepherd pushed some of the larger sheep away gently with his staff and raised up a young lamb. The animal's bright white coat shone under the midday sun.

Moses inspected every inch of the animal. "May I?" He reached out.

"It would be an honor." Kefir lifted the animal into his waiting arms.

He raised the animal slightly to check its underside and ran a hand over its coat. "Not a blemish on him."

The shepherd leaned on his staff. "He is magnificent."

"Here you are, sister." He offered the lamb to Miriam.

She cradled her arms to accept the animal. The weight made her arms buckle slightly. "Healthy little one too." She adjusted her stance to bear the additional weight.

Kefir chuckled. "Only the best for Moses' family."

The lamb nuzzled her chin.

"And so friendly." She closed her eyes and nuzzled him back. His young curls were the softest Miriam had ever felt. His clear black eyes stared up at her. He smelled of sand and fresh air.

"Thank you," Moses said with a wave.

"My pleasure," Kefir replied.

"Take him to my tent," Moses ordered. "I've got to meet with the elders."

Miriam walked toward the camp carrying the young lamb in her arms. His warmth felt good next to her skin.

When they arrived at the tent, she put the animal in the main area and tied him with a lead to the main post. She poured some fresh water in a bowl and put it near him.

"There you go little guy," she whispered.

The lamb lapped up the cool water in a hurry.

"I bet you're hungry too." She rummaged around the food storage. "I think I've got a manna cake around here somewhere, ah!" She reached for a wrapped bundle. "Here we are." She unwrapped the package and removed the top cake before returning it to its place.

She sat beside the lamb and broke off a little piece. "Here." She held it to him.

He sniffed it once and looked up at her.

"It's good." She broke off another piece and placed it in her mouth. "See."

She held out the small piece again.

His little pink tongue came out and licked the cake. Then his mouth opened and bit the morsel out of her fingers.

The crunch of the cake eased her concern that he might not take to living with them.

She broke off another small piece.

He bleated at her.

"Oh, here." She held an open palm out with the bite. "Healthy appetite too."

Miriam cared for the young lamb for the next few days. She made sure he had fresh water and something to eat. His playful bleating roused her to spend time petting and brushing him. His soft wool warmed her on the cool desert nights.

The morning light of the fourth day of tending to the lamb meant preparation for the coming night. She reached over and rustled the top patch of wool on the lamb's head.

He stirred and gave a soft bleat.

She chuckled as his little tongue extended with a yawn.

After changing dresses, she picked him up and took him into the front part of the tent. She tied his lead to the pole and retrieved a fresh bowl of water for him.

She hurried through collecting her manna and

making a few fresh cakes. Then she sat next to the lamb feeding him bites of her food.

"Today is the fourteenth day," Moses spoke as he moved around the tent. "Passover."

The word brought Miriam back a year ago to the time they prepared to leave Egypt. Visions of plagues filled her mind. People suffered under the judgment of God. Her own people prepared to escape. Her shoulders hung low as she remembered the weight of the pack on her back, waiting for their signal while they ate. Her heart raced and her hands shook. She didn't notice the lamb bleating at her for another bite.

Moses reached for her hand and gave it a squeeze. "Sister?"

She shook her thoughts clear and met his gaze.

"Remembering last time?" he tried.

She nodded embarrassed that her fear had pulled him away from his work.

"Steady." He patted her hand. "The past is behind us. This is simply to remind us."

"I know." She smiled up at him. "The memories are often still fresh in my dreams as if they happened yesterday."

"Dreams are often warnings draped in imaginary wrappings."

"Moses," a husky voice called outside the tent.

He ducked his head and went out.

Miriam followed.

Three men stood in front of them.

She recognized the oldest one as Shelumiel, the leader of the tribe of Simeon. His gray hair and worn face counted his age though he stood tall and strong with the weight of his tribe on his shoulders.

The other two were definitely brothers. They had similar chins and the same colored eyes. She recognized them as Gil and Jerah, the sons of Berel.

"These men have an issue I haven't been able to solve," Shelumiel explained. "I was hoping you could hear their trouble."

"Speak on," Moses said.

"This morning our father died and we buried him in the sands," Gil spoke.

"We know that tonight is the passover," Jerah added. "But since we have touched a dead body we have become unclean."

Moses nodded.

"Moses?" Aaron came out of the tent behind them.

"Brother," he welcomed him to the discussion. "It seems these men have become unclean by contact with a dead body. Yet they still wish to observe the passover tonight."

"Well, that can't be." Aaron spread his palms out. "The law you gave from the Lord was clear that no one who is unclean can be part of the passover."

"We would really like to be able to offer our contribution before the Lord today," Gil urged.

Moses rubbed his beard as he studied the sand. "Wait here." He met their anticipating glares. "I will hear what the Lord will command concerning you."

Moses and Aaron trekked toward the tabernacle.

Miriam stood with the men. "Sons of Berel?"

The two nodded.

"I'm sorry for your loss," she offered. "Your father was a good man."

Gil attempted a smile, but it was shadowed by sorrow.

"He was," Jerah responded.

"Would you mind if I visited your sister, Varda, tomorrow?"

"You have my permission," Gil answered.

"Thank you." Jerah shifted his weight.

"Don't worry," Miriam comforted. "Moses will ask and the Lord will answer."

Gil relaxed his shoulders and let out his breath.

Moses and Aaron's forms came back into view.

"I've heard from the Lord," Moses said. "If any man of you or any future generation shall be unclean by reason of a dead body or be in a journey far off, he may still keep the passover unto the Lord."

"Thank you." Gil bowed. "This means so much to our family."

"Go in peace," Moses offered.

The brothers turned toward their own tent.

"I will pass along the new command to the other leaders," Shelumiel said before leaving with a bow.

"Now." Moses put a hand on Aaron's shoulder. "Let's make our own preparations."

Miriam ducked into the tent. She saw the lamb still tied to the post. She loosed him and lifted him up into her arms. "Time to go."

She walked behind Moses and Aaron toward the tabernacle. She stopped at the door of the tabernacle while Moses and Aaron continued in.

Aaron joined his sons at the preparation tables while Moses came back to the door.

Miriam placed the lamb into his waiting arms. She watched hundreds of animals be slain on the sacrificial tables, but this felt different. Her eyes held the gaze of the young lamb.

Moses handed him to Aaron, who placed him on the nearest table.

He inspected the lamb before declaring it a clean sacrifice.

Miriam remembered why they had to kill the lambs. They were a substitute for the bearer's sins. The animals' blood would cover the darkness of their iniquities for another year so God's judgment would pass over them.

The memories of each of the plagues came flooding back to her. From the bloody river to the darkness that lasted three days. Each new plague was a reminder of God's judgment on Egypt. And the last one. The last one had been the hardest.

The sadness reflected in Puah's eyes came back to her and she grabbed hold of her chest. Though the midwife didn't lose a son to the last plague, she had lost many of those she had helped welcome into the world.

Miriam felt the sadness overwhelm her. Tears burned at her eyes. She missed her friend. Loneliness clawed at her insides.

Aaron prayed over the lamb.

The sons of Egypt had to die for their father's sins. She thought. *The animal offerings have to die because of our sins. My sin. That lamb has to die because of my sins.*

The weight of the realization sent her to her knees.

The perfect lamb has to die for me. She wailed inwardly.

Aaron lifted his sharpened knife to the lamb's throat and made a clean cut. He collected the blood into a bowl before expertly cleaning and dividing the animal being extra careful not to break any of the bones. He wrapped the pieces in a cloth and handed them to Moses.

Moses turned to the door of the tent. "Sister?" He rushed toward her.

Miriam saw the blood seep through the cloth.

"Are you ill?" He reached for her shoulder as he knelt beside her.

"My sin," she whimpered.

"What?" He examined her.

"My sin," she spoke clearer as she brushed her fingers over the blood spot on the cloth. "Mine. He had to die because of me."

Moses adjusted the package to his other arm and wrapped his free arm around her. "They have to die because of all of our sins so we can live."

She dried her tears and met his calm eyes.

"So we can live," he repeated.

For you. The whisper brought with it a wave of peace.

Moses stretched out a hand to help her rise.

She accepted the aid and then the bundle. Tucking it in close to her chest, she took a deep breath.

For you. She heard repeated on the wind.

Chapter 17

"And the cloud of the LORD was upon them by
day, when they went out of the camp."
-NUMBERS 10:34

1445 B.C.

On the twentieth day of the second month of the
second year after leaving Egypt, the cloud rose off
the tabernacle.

"Time to pack up," Moses shouted.

Miriam packed her things and went with the
other Levities to help load the pieces of the
tabernacle onto the carts. Two oxen were tied to
each cart ready to receive the pieces.

The Gershonites and Merarites had finished
disassembling the curtains and poles from the
outside courtyard and inner tent. They loaded
them on their carts.

Miriam looked at the fully loaded six carts.
"Where are they going to put all that's left?"

"On their shoulders," Moses said, standing

behind her.

She turned to look at him. "Surely there are other carts available to help."

"There are, but that's not what the Lord has commanded."

"How far are we traveling?"

He shrugged. "To wherever the cloud leads us."

"You expect them to carry all that on their backs the entire trip? And what of their own belongings?"

"Miriam," he said in his most tender voice. "This is the Lord's way, not ours. Sometimes it doesn't always make sense to us."

She looked at the men who helped lift each other's burdens onto their broad backs.

"They are strong men."

"We are strong too." She waved to the women with her. "Let us help."

He shook his head. "Only the men the Lord has called will carry the pieces."

"But Moses-"

"No, sister." He held up a hand. "I will not lose anyone else to disobedience."

She shut her mouth and held her tongue. Her jaw tightened as she looked at her family's men being weighed down like pack animals.

"If you really want to help." Moses sighed. "Have the women to help carry the men's personal items. We can spread the load around, so no one is too burdened."

"We can do that." She squared her shoulders.

"Have everyone help," he cautioned. "There are young and older men who could carry some more as well."

She nodded. "I'll get to it right away."

"Quick. We will be setting out soon."

When everyone was assigned and ready to go, Miriam made one last check with her brothers before heading to her spot in the march.

"We are ready to go," Moses told Aaron.

Eleazar and Ithamar took their place at the front of the ark ready to lift the gold staves upon their shoulders.

Miriam looked at Aaron, who stared at the two empty places on the backside of the ark.

Four sons to carry the ark, but only two remained.

Miriam realized why Moses warned her about obedience.

Moses put a hand on Aaron's shoulder. "Mishael. Elzaphan," he called.

The two men came to him.

"Take up the ark." He pointed to the two vacant spots.

They obeyed at once.

With a nod, Moses indicated to Aaron to hand Eleazar one of the silver trumpets the Lord requested to be made in order to signal the camp.

Eleazer licked his lips and lifted the end of the narrow tube to his mouth. The long blast was the sign for the eastern tribes to set out. He handed the instrument back to his father and lifted his portion of the golden stave onto his shoulder to raise the ark.

"Rise up, Lord," Moses shouted. "And let your enemies be scattered. Let them that hate You flee before You."

The tribes of Judah, Issachar, and Zebulun headed out behind the ark. Following them were the families of Gershonites and Merarites carrying the hangings of the tabernacle.

Miriam stood waiting. She adjusted the extra load between her shoulders.

In the distance, she heard the second blast signal the south tribes to set out. After them, the Kohathites were set to march.

Three days later, the cloud stood still in the wilderness of Paran.

"Return, Oh Lord, unto the many thousands of Israel," Moses shouted.

By the time Miriam's group made it to the front of where they stopped, the curtains of the outside courtyard were being raised. The inner tent had already been set up and ready for the pieces her family carried.

She helped unpack the Levites' belongings and set to work setting up her own tent for the very first time. As promised, her brother had adjusted the grouping to provide her enough space for her tent.

After she drove the last peg into the sand, she stood back to admire her hard work. The lines where she had sewn the goat's hair together were stitched strongly. She was sure they would hold against the winds of the desert. Hopefully, she wouldn't have to pitch this tent too many times. She wished they would soon be in Canaan and settled in a real home again.

She imagined a lovely stone building to care for all her own. Images of new rugs covering a real floor filled her heart with joy. Evenings sitting in her private open courtyard watching the stars stirred her soul.

With a lighter heart, she made her way north through the camp toward the tents of the tribe of Dan. Moses had instructed that the outsiders would travel and be collected under this tribe. This would include those who came with them from Egypt, those ill, and those who found themselves without families to care for them.

Miriam had inwardly praised God for

collecting the grouping. It was hard enough to visit as many widows as she could when they were scattered in the camp of over two million. This way she could easily keep track of those who needed her or the help of the midwives.

She left one tent, heading toward another when loud voices caught her attention.

"I miss meat," one spoke with such longing that it made Miriam's heart ached.

She recognized the voice as Tiye and moved toward her tent. The wealthy Egyptian woman had been left with her husband's wealth and no one to share it with. She tired of Pharaoh's rule and wanted to travel to unknown lands.

"We just had the passover lamb a few days ago," another voice answered. Onofria, a neighboring widow's speech was even.

"Once a year is not enough!" Tiye yelled.

Miriam moved closer to the tent from where the conversation flowed. She reached for the flap.

"The priests get to eat meat from the offerings and we are left to only eat manna," Tiye continued. "Even their women get to eat meat."

Miriam held her steps. Her cheeks burned.

"This journey was supposed to take a few weeks, but weeks have turned into months which have stretched to a year."

She held her breath and faltered. *Should I enter or leave?*

"We should have been feasting in Canaan already," the woman's accusations continued. "Not stuck out here starving in the wilderness."

Miriam took a few steps backward. Her heart hurt for the unhappiness seeping from the tent. She didn't know what to say to argue with the woman's words. They were true, but they still hurt.

It wasn't her idea to keep meat all to the Levities. She would have shared her portion if Moses had allowed. She remembered what it felt like to watch Aaron and his sons feast for a straight week on the first offerings when they became priests.

Fire flashed around her and caught her attention. The strikes lit the tent in front of her and burned it to the ground within moments.

Miriam looked around to see the charred bodies of those who were speaking. The smell of burning flesh assaulted her nose and she covered her face with her headcloth. She turned on the scene.

She ran toward the tabernacle as flashes of fire sparked like lightning around her. Tent after tent caught the flames and burned as she passed.

People in nearby tents went running in different directions. Men rushed to stomp out the fires so they would not spread to their own tents.

Miriam hurried straight to the gate of the

tabernacle. "Moses!" she yelled. "Moses!"

He came to her. "Sister?"

"Fire from the Lord," she panted. "It's on the outside of the camp."

More women and men came running behind her.

"Fire!" an older woman yelled.

"Help us, Moses!" a man cried out.

"I will pray." Moses raised his hands to calm the people.

He went into the inner tent for several moments.

Miriam couldn't turn behind her even though she could still hear the echoes of screams and chaos from the edges of the camp.

When Moses reappeared and walked toward them, the noise ceased.

"The Lord has answered," he said. "The fire is quenched."

The people thanked Moses and returned to clean up the mess.

"What happened out there?" Moses asked Miriam as he took her elbow.

"I was visiting some of the widows and I overheard some speaking. They were complaining about not having meat to eat."

"I hope they have learned their lesson now not to press the Lord."

"Me too." Miriam returned to her tent for the

day.

The next morning, she went back to the outskirt group. She still had people to check on and even more after the fires.

"I was trying to put out the fire in the tent," Chione explained as Miriam wrapped her burn. "It would have destroyed everything…" Her breathing caught. "I've already lost so much…" She wept.

"Shh, there now," Miriam comforted. "Let's get you taken care of."

When she finished with Chione, she went into the tent of Edrice.

"Welcome," the young Egyptian woman greeted her.

"I came to check in on you," Miriam returned her greeting.

"Did you see what happened yesterday?"

Miriam folded inward in despair. "I was here when it started."

"So awful."

She nodded.

"Still, I know how they felt."

Miriam lifted her head in confusion.

"This time of year would find the banks of the Nile overflowing with fish." Her glare was a few thousand miles away back in Egypt. "The thought of it makes my mouth water."

"Edrice, please don't speak of such things,"

Miriam looked up waiting for the fire to start again.

"Oh." She looked up too. "I supposed you're right."

Miriam walked through the group of tents. She was weary and worn. Each woman wanted to recount the previous day's event over and over. Her heart ached over the loss of life and the stirring it caused among the people who trusted the Hebrews enough to follow them.

"Remember the cucumbers?" Husani's voice made her perk up.

"I had one once that was as big around as my arm," Seb remarked.

"And melons the size of your head."

"That rich soil of the Nile was perfect for growing crops."

"Leeks, onions, garlic, remember all the fresh greens?"

"Yes, and what do we have now?"

"Manna," they answered together.

"Gather and grind, beat it and bake it. Day in and day out." Husani's voice carried dread and hardness.

Miriam picked up the hem of her dress to rush back toward the safety of her tent, but hesitated when she saw Moses standing nearby.

"Moses?" She came up to him.

He pressed a finger over his lips.

Miriam stood still listening.

"When are we going to have meat?" someone in another tent asked.

"Remember fishing all day long?" another voice carried to her ears.

Murmurs surrounded her as she listened. She looked to Moses. His eyes flared as he turned away. She followed him all the way into his tent.

He hit his knees on the rug and covered his face. "Why have You afflicted your servant?" he prayed. "Why have I not found favor in your sight? Why have you laid the burden of these people upon me?"

Miriam pressed herself up against the tent wall.

"Have I given birth to all these people that I am responsible for them as a mother? Where am I going to get flesh enough to feed them all because they weep all night saying, 'Give us flesh to eat.' I am not able to bear all these people alone. This is too hard for me." He buried his face in the carpet.

She wanted to reach for her brother to comfort him, but she stood still.

"If this is how you are going to deal with me, then go ahead and kill me."

Miriam's knees buckled and she fell on them.

"If I have not found favor in your sight, then let me not see my evil."

Tears streamed down her cheeks. She crawled

next to her brother and waited in the stillness.

When he leaned up, she matched his movement.

"The Lord has answered," he said.

Miriam saw his eyes were red to match his cheeks. He had been crying as well. She waited for him to continue.

"I need to gather seventy men out of our officers and bring them to the tabernacle."

She nodded.

He patted her back. "Don't worry, sister. The Lord still has much to say."

She hugged his neck. *Don't leave me.* The words of her heart cried in silence. *I couldn't bear to lose you too.*

Miriam walked with her brother and stood at the gate of the tabernacle.

Moses had set each of the elders around the outside. They all prayed aloud.

A wind blew strong over them. A cloud rested upon Moses and then moved to sit on each of the men he had gathered. As the cloud moved, their prayers turned into prophecies.

"Sanctify yourselves," Moses's voice carried over the men speaking. It wasn't precisely his voice. It was deeper and stronger. "Tomorrow you will eat flesh for you have cried into the ears of the Lord. You will not just eat for one day or two or even for a week, but for an entire month you will eat flesh until it comes out of your nose. You will eat so much flesh that it will become repugnant to you because you have despised the Lord who is among you."

"But Lord," Moses' voice changed into a softer and recognizable quality. "The battle men alone are over six hundred thousand. How will I give them meat for an entire month? Even if we slay every one of the flocks and herds we brought out of Egypt and collect all the fish in the sea, there would not be enough to feed everyone."

"Is My hand so short that I can't reach and do this thing?" his voice changed into the deeper tone. "You will see whether My word shall come to pass or not."

"Moses," Nahshon called out to him.

Moses turned his attention to the Judah leader.

"There are two in the camp, Eldad and Medad. The cloud came and rested upon them and they are prophesying as well, but they are not here at the tabernacle with you."

"Give orders that they cease," Joshua demanded.

"Are you envious for my sake?" Moses asked. "I wish all the Lord's people were prophets and that the Lord would put His spirit upon all of them."

Joshua held his peace, but Miriam could see his jaw tighten.

She listened to all the prophecies flow one over another. Promises of hope and plans for the future mingled in her ears. The waves of presence and peace filled her to the point she thought if she opened her mouth, she too would join the men. Her foot tapped a new beat in the sand. She longed to grab her timbrel and add to the glory around her, but dared not move for fear of missing one word.

Then a great wind blew from the direction of the sea. Quail pressed into the camp to the point where Miriam could not see the end of them on the horizon. She couldn't walk without tripping on piles of birds.

The smell of them brought back the memory of the night she had feasted on them too abundantly. Her stomach turned.

Leaders from every tribe and family group set out to collect their harvest.

Miriam witnessed them returning from their collection after two days of gathering. Men hauled carts filled with dead quail back to their tribe tents and dispersed them among their people.

For several nights, she watched women lay birds outside their tents and cover them with salt as they had done fish and other meat in Egypt.

"They still don't trust him," Eliora said, standing beside Miriam.

She shook her head. "I don't know if they ever

will."

Noises rustled around them.

They exchanged a glance.

"What is that?" Eliora asked.

She shrugged.

People came out of their tents throwing up. Their skin was pale and they were sweating.

Eliora rushed to the nearest person asking for information.

The woman couldn't talk through the regurgitated meat.

She held the woman's hair out of her face.

"What's is it?" Miriam asked, rushing to her side.

"Look." Eliora nodded to the pile. "They are acting like a bunch of wild animals. They're not even chewing the meat all the way."

"She's choking?"

Eliora opened the woman's mouth. "I don't see any obstruction."

Another handful of people came out of their tents into the open space to vomit.

"Should I go get Moses?" Miriam stood.

"Hurry," the midwife urged.

She returned with her brother as quickly as she could.

"Look." She waved to the growing group of people sick to their stomachs. "It is as I said."

"Is the meat poisoned?" Moses asked.

"I think it's worse than that," Eliora said coming up to them wiping her hand on a cloth. "I've spoken to several of them and I think there is a simple explanation."

He waved her on.

"They are making themselves sick on the quail."

"How can that be?" He glanced around.

"It's all their eating. I've asked several of them and they've all given similar answers." She wrapped her arms around herself. "They've stopped eating manna and are gorging themselves simply on meat. It's not good for their stomachs."

"We are not ill," Miriam said.

"The Levities are more used to having meat in their diets. Your tribe eats of the offerings, correct?"

Moses nodded.

"These people only get meat once a year and in small quantities. For the past few days they've overloaded their systems with it and their bodies are rejecting it."

"What do we do?"

"Tell them to slow down and add manna back into their meals. They've got to stop overeating or they will die."

At the end of a month, Miriam stood with Eliora over a fresh set of new sand piles.

"You were right," she told her young friend.

"They simply wouldn't stop." Tears rolled down her sandy cheeks.

Moses came upon them and shook his head. "We shall call this place, Kibrothhattaavah."

"Graves of lust," Miriam interpreted. "How appropriate."

Two men moved to cover the last grave.

Miriam saw Moses close his eyes and a single tear roll down his cheek.

She looked back to the wrapped body. Under the grave clothes lay her sister-in-law, Zipporah. She had grown ill as many of the rest, but didn't recover. Elisheba found her before sunrise.

Miriam placed a hand on her brother's back. "She was a good woman."

Moses opened his eyes and glanced down at her with a slight nod.

She rubbed her face against his arm. *How many more do we have to bury, Lord?*

Chapter 18

"And Miriam and Aaron spake against Moses because of the Ethiopian woman whom he had married: for he had married an Ethiopian woman."
-NUMBERS 12:1

Miriam pounded the last tent peg into the sands of Hazeroth. She reached for her bag of personal items when something caught her eye. She stood tall and peered around the other tent blocking her view.

Her heart accelerated as she caught a glimpse of Elisheba driving in the last peg for the tent of Aaron. Moses had also agreed that they needed a place of their own. Each of the siblings were finally spreading their tents wide like fresh wings of baby birds. She waved.

Elishia returned the gesture and made her way into her tent.

Miriam squinted against the bright sun as she looked around at the camp filling in around her.

Suddenly, Moses' form came into view about a stone's throw away and she noticed someone was walking with him. She considered the person had come to him seeking advice, but her heart skipped a beat when she noticed the form was obviously feminine.

She stepped closer.

The two walked at a slow pace deep in private conversation.

The nearer Miriam came, the more the female became clear. She had seen the woman before. Tharbis. Her full form was accentuated by the ties in her ornate dress. Her dark skin shone and her features were set nicely.

She was a Cushite from Egypt. She had been taken from her homeland and set to work as a slave for the Egyptians. When they left Egypt, the woman claimed to believe in God and was welcomed to join the exodus. She lived outside the tents of Dan with a group of former slaves.

Moses came upon his tent and held the flap open for her.

Tharbis ducked inside and he followed her.

What could be the meaning of this? Miriam felt heat rise in her cheeks.

She rushed to the tabernacle but halted her steps at the gate. She searched the group of similarly dressed priests until she found the one she was looking for.

"Aaron," she called to him.

Her brother turned. "Sister, are you well?"

"I'm not sure."

He stepped closer to meet her at the opening. "Are you ill?"

"Nothing like that."

People bringing their offerings pushed by them.

"Can this wait until tonight?" he asked, receiving a lamb. "We are very busy."

She pressed closer to him. "I don't think this can wait."

Aaron handed the animal to Eleazer. "What is it that had gotten you riled so?"

"It's Moses."

"Is he ill?"

"No." She huffed. "No one is ill. Unless he has an illness of the mind. Which is the only explanation for such behavior."

"Speak clearer, sister," Aaron warned.

"I was pitching my tent when I saw Moses enter his with a woman."

"Who?"

"Tharbis."

"The Cushite?"

She nodded.

"He has taken her as his wife." He received another lamb and passed it off to his son.

"What?"

"He told me of his intentions as we marched."

"How could you agree to this?" She stomped her foot.

"He didn't ask my permission. She has no family to ask."

"Doesn't he follow his own laws?" she crossed her arms. "Did he say something about not taking women from other cultures."

"Officially, she is one of ours," he explained. "She has claimed to follow our God from the time we left Egypt."

"But she is not an Israelite by birth." She paced a small circle in the sand. "Has God only spoke to Moses?"

Aaron raised a bushy brow.

"Has he not spoken to us as well?"

A man waiting to hand over his offering looked Miriam up and down.

Two women in line behind him gasped and whispered to each other.

"God has spoken to all three of us," Aaron agreed, lowering his voice. "What does that have to do with this woman?"

"As two of the three authorities, we should have been consulted in this matter." She tightened her grip on her arms. "How are the people to take Moses' leadership seriously when Zipporah's body is in the ground less than a week and he has already married some outsider."

"Eleazer," Aaron called to his son.

"Yes?"

"Will you please take my place." He waved to the line that grew at the gate. "I will return shortly."

Eleazer nodded and accepted the next person's offering.

"Let's go speak with Moses." Aaron grabbed Miriam's arm and turned her around.

The two found Moses standing outside his tent with the woman in question.

"Brother." Miriam marched straight up to him. "We need a word with you."

"And what word would that be?" Moses teased.

"This is a very serious matter." She straightened. "Not a time to be joking."

"Miriam." Aaron scowled.

"He takes none of this seriously," she whined.

"Take what seriously?" Moses asked, passing a glance between the two of them.

"Do you deny taking that woman as your wife?" Miriam accused.

"Tharbis?" Moses asked. "Why, yes, she is my wife now."

"And you felt no need to take counsel with Aaron and myself in this matter?"

Moses eyed his sister. "It was my decision to make."

"She is an outsider."

"She worships the Lord. She is welcomed here as one of us."

"Then why does she dwell with those who live on the outskirts of our camp?"

Moses looked behind himself to his tent. "She lives with me."

"She is a Cushite!" Miriam hurled at him.

"She is a follower of the Lord," he answered with all the calmness of a windless day. "Her heritage does not exclude that fact."

"You are one of the leaders of the Israelites," she whipped. "What you do is judged by all."

"What I do is judged by the Lord." He took a breath before continuing, "My former wife is dead. Would you rather I not marry again and live in loneliness?"

"I'd rather you would have discussed this with Aaron and myself so we could have directed you to a nice *Hebrew* woman," she emphasized the word. "We are your older siblings after all."

"But not my parents." He looked at Aaron, who remained silent. "I am over eighty years old and free to make my own choices of whom I marry."

"You are breaking the law you brought us from God," Miriam pleaded.

"I've broken no law."

"Moses! Aaron! Miriam!" a clear and robust voice boomed around them.

Miriam looked to Aaron who looked to Moses.

"All three of you come to the tabernacle."

She glanced around for the source of the voice.

"It was the Lord," Moses answered her silent question.

"How did I hear it?"

"I heard it too," Aaron said.

"I don't think that means anything good," Moses answered. "We need to obey His call."

The three siblings made their way to the tabernacle and stood in the courtyard.

"Father," Eleazer said. "What is going on?"

"Clear the people to make room for us."

He nodded and led people away from the courtyard.

A pillar of cloud came down and stood at the door to the inner tent.

"Come forward," the loud voice called from the cloud.

The three siblings came close.

"Now, hear My words," the voice continued. "If there be a prophet among you I, the Lord, will make Myself known unto him in a vision and will speak to him in a dream."

Miriam's skin tingled as a flood of mixed dreams invaded her mind.

"Though this is not how I speak with My servant, Moses, who is faithful in all My house."

The cloud crackled with lightning and thunder

as it had when it covered the mountain.

"With Moses, I speak mouth to mouth. I do not speak in riddles and hidden speech. He has seen My likeness. Why then are you not afraid to speak against My servant?" A loud crackle popped from the cloud and thunder shook the ground.

The cloud lifted up and left.

Gasps came from behind them.

Miriam looked at the crowd who had backed away. Then she turned to look at Aaron and Moses.

Both of her brother's eyes were wide with fear.

She turned her gaze on herself. She stretched out her arms. Her beautiful olive complexion was now as white as the manna that frosted the ground every morning. She put her hands to her cheeks and rubbed. Her skin was rough and bumpy.

She looked back at her brothers. Her breath was near a pant.

"My master." Aaron fell at Moses' feet. "I beg you not to lay this sin upon us. We have done foolishly and we have sinned against you." He reached for his brother's foot and kissed it. "Don't leave her as a dead one."

Moses looked to the sky and cried out, "Lord, heal her now. Oh God, I beg you."

Miriam kept her eyes on the backs of her hands, waiting for their normal color to return. They didn't change.

"If she had dishonored her father, would she not be ashamed for seven days?" the voice boomed. "Shut her out of the camp for seven days and then afterward she may be received in again."

She looked up at her brother and shook her head. "Please, no," she mouthed.

Moses turned his back to her. "Eleazer, escort her to the outskirts. Find her a place there."

Aaron rose to his feet and stood next to Moses with his back to her as well.

"Brothers." She reached out for them.

Eleazar grabbed her wrist and led her away from the tabernacle.

She pulled against him. The open sores on her skin burned with the movement.

"Please," she pleaded. "Don't send me away." She dug her heels into the sand and stretched for her brothers.

They didn't turn toward her.

"Release me, nephew," she attempted to order Eleazer.

He continued to lead her to the outskirts of the camp and didn't remove his grip until they came to their destination.

They stood in front of a plain tent.

"You are to remain here," he said, making his voice deep with authority. "Don't make this harder on them."

She opened her mouth to object, but thought

better. Clenching her jaw, she nodded.

He turned and left her.

Miriam faced the opening and sighed. She glared down at her skin and wept.

When she had dried her tears with the back of her sleeve, she stepped into the tent.

A head rose from a mat at the back of the room.

"Miriam?" a soft voice called.

"Zeruah," her voice shook.

The woman rose to meet her. "What is-" A gasp caught the rest of her question.

Miriam ducked her head as fresh tears blurred her sight.

"What happened?" She reached for her arm and examined the spots.

"I've been plagued."

Zeruah pulled her in close.

Miriam glanced at the bandages that covered the woman's arms. She had come many times to this tent to bring food and provisions to those who found themselves in need to heal. She never dreamed she would be an occupant. The weight of her sickness crashed over her and she buried her face into Zeruah's dress to weep again.

Chapter 19

"And Miriam was shut out from the camp seven days: and the people journeyed not till Miriam was brought in again."
-NUMBERS 12:15

Miriam rolled over again on the thin blanket, desperate to find a comfortable position in which to escape into slumber. Much to her despair, none was to be found.

She sighed and sat up. The open sores protested all over her body. Pulling her knees up to her chest, Miriam gently touched the hastily wrapped wounds on her hands as she began to weep quietly.

"Miriam?"

"I'm alright." She sniffled. "Go back to sleep, Zeruah."

The woman who shared the tent pulled herself over. "You're obviously not all right or you'd be asleep."

"How can anyone here be okay?" She let the

burning tears fall freely.

Zeruah was silent.

"I'm sorry. It's just…"

"No, you're right. We're not okay, but that doesn't mean we should give up."

As Miriam's eyes adjusted to the darkness, she saw Zeruah watching her.

"Do you think you are ready to talk about it?" The woman asked as she pulled a blanket over her shoulders to shut out the coolness of the desert night.

"Do you think it will help?"

"Couldn't hurt." She smiled. "Maybe talking will help ease your mind enough to go back to sleep."

"Maybe."

"I'm not forcing you, but I'm here if you want to talk. I don't think I'm going back to sleep any time soon."

Miriam shifted a little. "My brother married a Cushite."

"And that bothered you?"

"She wasn't a Hebrew. I mean his last wife was at least a Midianite. I lived with that union and held my tongue, for the most part. But…a Cushite?" Miriam rose and paced around the small tent. "There was no benefit to Moses in the arrangement, not at all. I honestly thought the man had lost his mind."

"But wasn't that his choice?"

Miriam stopped. "Well, yes." She started walking again. "It's not a private matter for Moses. Everything he does affects this entire group of people."

"Do you think this woman is dangerous?"

Miriam shrugged as she sat down beside her. "Not really, I guess."

"So, what exactly bothered you?"

She thought about the question. "She is so different. She's not a Hebrew. She's not like us. And she's a Cushite!" Miriam jumped up and paced the cramped quarters again.

"Are you trying to tell me the only thing you have against this woman is her nationality?"

She huffed.

"Did you even get to know her?"

"Moses didn't give us a chance! He turned around and married her without our permission."

"Did he need it?"

"No." Miriam crossed her arms. "But…"

"But what?" The woman patted the ground next to herself. "Sit down. You're making me dizzy."

She obeyed.

"Now, speak honestly with me. What is really bothering you?"

She bit her lower lip. "She's different."

"You mean her skin?"

Miriam looked at the dirt and then nodded slowly.

"That's what all of this is about? Just because she's dark skinned?"

"What are the people supposed to think of a leader who marries someone like her?"

"He cares for her, perhaps?"

She flinched.

"Miriam?"

"Yes!" She unfolded her arms. "I have a problem with her because of her skin color. Moses should be the example. If he goes around making bad choices, then we all suffer."

"I hate to tell you this, but the only one suffering in this situation is you."

She looked up into Zeruah's eyes.

"Give me your hand."

Miriam extended her arm.

She gently unwrapped one of the bandages.

Miriam turned away in disgust.

"Look at your arm."

She glanced down quickly and then away again.

"No, Miriam, really look."

She fought the lurch of her stomach at the scent which came from her own exposed skin and turned to glare at her limb.

The slowly rising sun poured light into the tent.

"What color is your arm?"

"It's white!" Miriam gasped.

"That's right. Because of your sinful pride against someone else's skin color, God has turned your skin white. Not even the white of fresh snow, but the white of a dead body. Your skin is now an offense even to yourself."

"I never thought about it like that before." She drew the sore-covered arm into her chest.

"Are you ready to tell me the rest?"

She nodded. "Aaron and I went to Moses. We were… *I* was furious. I rashly hurled insults at my own brother and his new wife. In front of everyone, I questioned if God had only spoken to Moses, but claimed He had also spoken to Aaron and myself."

"Ouch."

"I was so angry with Moses."

"What did he say?"

"That's just it." She recovered the sore on her arm. "He didn't say anything. He just stood there…taking it all." Miriam flinched at the hurt she remembered seeing on her brother's face. "Then we heard it…"

"Heard what?"

"God. His voice was so clear. He called our names and then told us to go to the tabernacle. The closer we got, the cloud pillar came down in front of the door to the inner tent. I've never been more frightened in all my life. Then the Lord spoke to us from the cloud.

"He said that Moses was the one He had chosen to speak clearly with even though Aaron and I also hear through dreams and visions. He asked why I wasn't afraid to speak out against the one He had chosen. Then the cloud moved to cover my brothers and me. When it moved away, I heard Aaron gasp. I looked down at my arms." She rubbed her covered arm. "There were all these spots. Moses ordered me to the outskirts. As my nephew pulled me away, I heard Aaron whisper to Moses the word…Leprosy."

"I see," Zeruah empathized.

"I watched my brothers turn their backs on me." She wept. "All I could do was think about the day so long ago when I saw Moses' sweet face placed into the basket mother had made for him. Watching Mother put him in the river was the hardest thing I had ever done. But I knew I had to believe that God was going to take care of him. Now, the same trusting eyes had looked at me as if I were a monster."

"And so, you were banished here?"

"Yes." She wiped her tears on the back of her sleeve. "Moses had not said a single word up till then. He didn't say anything to our accusations and had not said anything when the Lord poured out His anger on us."

"But he spoke then?" Zeruah asked.

"Moses cried unto the Lord begging Him to heal me. I'll never forget those words." Tears fell again. "He was asking the only One who could heal me to go ahead and heal me. Even after everything I had said to him."

Zeruah wiped her wet eyes with a rag. "But God didn't."

She shook her head. "The last word from God was to shut me out of the camp for seven days."

"Then all is not lost for you."

Miriam lifted her head.

"God has said it will only last a week."

"When have you ever heard of Leprosy only lasting a week?"

"When have you ever heard of God lying?" She rose an eyebrow.

"Miriam?" a voice called outside the tent.

"Here."

Eliora poked her head in. "May I?"

"Come." She waved.

The midwife entered and knelt before them. "Your brother told me what happened.'

Miriam recoiled.

"I came to check on you."

"Why would you make yourself unclean to tend to me?"

"I'm a midwife. I practically live in a constant state of uncleanness."

"What about your guild? They need your leadership."

"One of the best things about leadership is having the ability to delegate."

Miriam smiled.

"Let me see that." She pointed to Miriam's arm.

She held it out.

"Good thing I brought some fresh bandages." The midwife clicked her tongue. "We wouldn't want you to get an infection."

Miriam's cheeks burned. "I tried to wrap them myself late last night."

"It shows," she teased. The midwife set to work removing the old bandages and cleaning the wounds.

"Eliora?" she whispered.

"Yes?"

"Thank you." She met her eyes and smiled. "I'm glad you're here."

"I brought some food too." She nodded to her other bag.

Zeruah reached for it and nibbled on the offerings.

"You'll need your strength to heal."

Miriam's smile turned sideways. "Will you come back?"

"As often as I can."

She sighed with relief.

Chapter 20

"This shall be the law of the leper in the day of
his cleansing: He shall be brought unto the
priest."
-LEVITICUS 14:2

Eliora returned two days later to check on
Miriam's bandages. She turned her arm over as
she examined her work.

"Any improvement?" Miriam asked.

The midwife checked each spot again.
"Everything looks the same."

"Oh." She hung her head.

"That's a good thing."

She lifted her glance.

"At least there are no signs of infection."

Miriam endured the scrubbing. "How come it
doesn't hurt?"

"It kills your senses." Eliora applied her special
balm to the spot she had just wiped clean. "That's
part of the danger."

"Danger?"

"Not just from infection, but if you don't realize an area is hurting, it could lead to loss."

"Loss?" The unsettling words kept a tight grip on her chest.

"If you injured your foot you'd feel it, right?"

She nodded.

"Then you'd be able to care for it. But what would happen if you didn't feel it?"

She thought about the possibilities. "It would continue on injured."

"And eventually may have to be removed."

The thoughts of missing fingers or a foot shook Miriam.

The midwife finished redressing each sore. "There we are."

"Thanks." Miriam pulled her wrapped arm toward her chest.

"You next." She reached for Zeruah.

The women blinked back confusion.

Eliora put a hand on her thin hip. "Do you think I only provide my services to the royal?" She winked at Miriam.

Zeruah chuckled and extended her arms.

"Any news?" Miriam asked.

"Nothing new."

"Have you spoken to my brothers?"

She shook her head. "Not since they told me you were here."

Miriam picked apart a manna cake.

"The whole camp seems to be stuck."

"Stuck?" Her head came up at the word.

The midwife hesitated as she wrapped the last spot on Zeruah's leg. "Like everyone is waiting on something."

"They are," Zeruah offered.

Eliora glanced to Miriam and then back to the woman. "What?"

"Miriam."

The sixth night Miriam sat starting at the Egyptian rug under her feet.

"Your seven days are almost up." Zeruah knelt beside her.

"Even if it does happen like that I'm not so sure I want to go back."

Zeruah tilted her head. "Why would you want to continue to live like this?"

"Because I deserve it." She met her curious gaze. "I see that now. For all my sin against both my brothers. I deserve to be like a dead one. I deserve to be banished from my family and my people to suffer for my sin."

Zeruah peered out of the tent flap and then sat back on her heels. "We haven't moved in all this time."

"So?" She looked up. "Sometimes we stay in one place for a while."

"True. But God hasn't had us move since you became leprous."

She shrugged.

"Do you believe God to be gracious and merciful?

She nodded.

"Then maybe He is waiting for your time to be completed before we move."

Miriam looked around. "Maybe you're right."

"I know I am."

Early the next morning, Miriam sat outside the small tent contemplating the last week. She thought of her brothers and what she would say if she did see them again.

Against the blinding sun, she saw a figure come toward her.

As he drew closer, Miriam stood to her feet and whispered, "Aaron."

Zeruah came out of the tent and followed her gaze. "He's coming for you."

"But I'm not ready."

"I don't think that matters." She went back into the tent.

Aaron drew close to Miriam.

"Aaron, I-"

He held up a hand.

She held her peace.

He stepped closer and reached for her hand.

"Aaron, don't…" She pulled her arm back.

He held up his hand again. Then he extended her arm and began to unwrap the bandages.

"Aaron, please don't…" Miriam wept.

He glanced quickly into her eyes and then back down to his work. He picked up her other arm and unwrapped it as well.

Tears blurred her vision.

Aaron twisted her arms around to examine them.

"Aaron, I'm so sorry." She caught his eyes.

He nodded down to her arms.

She glanced quickly and then brought her arms up to her face. "The sores are gone," Miriam gasped.

Aaron motioned her to follow him.

Miriam took one step and then turned back. She poked her head into the tent. "Zeruah," she called.

The woman came close to the opening.

She showed off the freshly healed skin and how the beautiful olive color had returned to her flesh.

"I knew God would heal you just as He said He would."

"Thank you, sweet friend."

Zeruah smiled. "Now, I don't want to see you back here again."

"I'll be praying for God to heal you."

Zeruah nodded. "Thank you."

Miriam followed Aaron back to the camp in silence.

They made their way to the tabernacle where Miriam saw all the offerings laid out on her behalf. Two clean birds were held in a cage with cedarwood, scarlet, and hyssop lay on the table next to it.

Aaron took one of the birds and killed it while Eleazer poured water over the creature. Then Aaron took the other bird and pieces of sacrifice and dipped them in the blood of the dead bird. Using each piece, he sprinkled Miriam with the blood seven times as he pronounced her clean.

When he was done, Aaron took the live bird out into the nearby field and released it. And upon returning to the tent, he pointed Miriam over to where Elisheba was waiting for her.

She attempted a slight grin which her sister-in-law met with an understanding nod.

In silence, she helped Miriam undress and wash her clothes. The two worked to shave the hair off Miriam's body. She thought she would feel saddened watching all the hair fall around her. But in a strange way, she felt relieved and refreshed by the process. The woman helped Miriam wipe herself clean from the loose hair, dress in fresh clothes, and then escorted her back to Aaron.

Two clean lambs, one ewe lamb, fine flour mixed with oil, and one log of oil were all waiting for her. Aaron accepted the offerings and placed them before the Lord. Taking a bowl of blood in his hands, Aaron walked over to Miriam. He dipped his fingers in the blood and marked her right ear, right thumb and then bent down and marked the big toe on her right foot.

Aaron took some oil and stretched Miriam's left arm out. Pouring the oil on the palm of her left hand, he then sprinkled the oil seven times before the Lord. With the remaining oil, he marked her right ear, thumb, and toe. Then he held the bowl over her head and poured the rest of the oil on her.

The cool oil ran down her shaven head and dripped down her body. She deeply inhaled the aroma. Its sweet scent relaxed her whole body.

Aaron killed the meat offering and burned the sacrifice on the altar before the Lord.

When he was done, he came close to Miriam and pronounced, "You are now clean."

Miriam couldn't help herself. She reached up and hugged her brother. "I'm so sorry, Aaron."

He nodded with a wide smile.

Miriam turned around to see the face of her

other brother. Her hands flew to her mouth. "Moses." She ran into his waiting arms.

As she nuzzled her oil-covered head into his tunic, she whispered, "Oh brother, please forgive me."

Moses rubbed her oily head and then pressed his forehead against hers. "All is forgiven."

She pulled him in close again and let her salty tears mix with the oil.

Chapter 21

"And Moses sent them to spy out the land of Canaan…"
-NUMBERS 13:17

Miriam raised her head covering against the wind to stop the sandy pieces from irritating her freshly shorn head. She rubbed the spots where her eyebrows used to be and felt slightly raised bumps.

"It won't be long before it all grows back," Eliora comforted. She looped her hand through Miriam's arm and rested her chin on her shoulder.

The two stood near the gate of the outer courtyard watching the cloud pillar dance above the inner tent.

"I know." Miriam sighed. "God's ways of teaching humility are sometimes extreme."

"The question is, did you learn the lesson?"

She rolled her eyes. "And then some."

"What was it like?" Eliora wondered.

"Hmm?"

"To hear His voice?"

"Frightening." She paused. "Yet, so familiar. It

was as if I'd heard the voice all my life."

"In your dreams."

She nodded then pointed to her chest. "And in here."

The cloud lifted off the inner tent and moved toward the north.

"Guess it's time to start packing again." Eliora unhooked her arm.

"She was right," Miriam whispered.

"Who?"

"Zeruah. She said the cloud wasn't moving because I was outside the camp. And that when I received my healing, we would move again."

Eliora looked to the cloud and back to her. "God shows favor even when we are disobedient."

"I suppose you're right, as well." She smiled at her friend.

"Has she improved?"

Miriam shook her head.

"I'll continue to keep an eye on her," she promised.

Her heart felt a little lighter. She wished her new friend's skin disease would be over as soon as hers, but Zeruah had been in the tent outside the camp a long time. "I pray for her all the time."

"As do I," Eliora added.

She hugged her friend. "Let's go pack."

It was only a matter of a few hours before Miriam took her place among the other

Kohathites in preparation to march. Her tent was easy to tear down alone and her burden seemed effortless. Her muscles ached to move after sitting in a tent with little to do for a week. She was ready to march.

They were coming close to Canaan and her senses tingled with the thought of laying under a solid roof once more. Perhaps their days of wandering were finally coming to a close.

After a short march, they stopped to reassemble the camp.

Miriam went to see Moses.

"Why have we stopped short?" she asked. "Canaan is just over the Jordan."

"The Lord has instructed us to spy out the land." He held the tent flap open for her to follow him out. "I'm sending word for Aaron to call the tribes together at the gate so everyone can hear the Lord's plan."

She followed him to the tabernacle as the signal of the silver trumpet sounded through the air.

Moses stood outside the gate as he spoke, "The Lord has commanded me to take twelve men, one from each tribe to spy out the land of Canaan."

Murmurs flew around the gathering.

"Shammua, Shaphat, Caleb, Igal, Joshua, Palti, Gaddiel, Gaddi, Ammiel, Sethur, Nahbi, and Geuel."

As he called each name, the men stepped forward.

"These will go into the mountains and spy out the land to gather information. We shall know from their report whether the people be strong or weak, few or many. And we shall know whether the land in which they dwell is a good one and how their cities are built."

He lowered his gaze to the men. "Be of good courage and bring back the fruit of the land."

The crowd cheered.

Moses stretched out a hand and placed it on Joshua's massive shoulder. "Lead them well," he encouraged.

"May I bring honor to the Lord," Joshua answered.

For forty days, the camp continued life as usual waiting for the twelve spies to return. Miriam visited the women on the outlying tents outside Dan's tribal grouping as much as she could. Her thankful heart refreshed her old bones to serve others once more.

"All these men seem to take a month to return from anything," Eliora complained to Miriam.

They had shared a midday meal and were

busying their hands as they waited for the day to cool outside.

Miriam chuckled as she tightened the stitch in the rug in her hand. "Imagine if my brother had sent twelve women."

"We would have been back two weeks ago not only with a detailed report of the land, but would have cooked up a hearty meal for our men in waiting." The midwife squared her shoulders.

She laughed so hard, her side ached. "I'm sure they'll return soon."

"I hope so." Eliora looked at the tent opening.

"Missing a particular one of them?" she teased.

The midwife blushed and set her eyes on her work. "I just can't bear the thought of Joshua out there among the enemy."

"He's led men into battle before," Miriam offered. "Besides, they aren't going into battle."

Eliora perked up.

"It's just a survey mission."

She stitched a few more rows. "I wonder what the people are like."

Miriam shrugged. "I've never met anyone from Canaan."

"Do you think they're as bad as everyone says." She swallowed hard.

"How do you mean?" Miriam set her work down in her lap.

"I've heard stories that they sacrifice their

children to appease their gods."

Miriam's mind gave her an all too real image of what that might look like. She shook it away. "Everyone believes different things."

"I-"

A long trumpet blast interrupted her.

"That's the signal to gather." Miriam set aside her rug. "The twelve must be back."

Eliora left her sewing on the floor and rushed toward the tabernacle.

Miriam hurried after her, but didn't try to keep pace with the woman who was less than half her age.

She found her friend at the back of the gathering straining to see over the crowd.

"I can get you closer," Miriam offered, standing beside her.

Eliora's wide eyes were all the answer she needed.

She looped her friend's arm in hers and stepped further toward Moses and Aaron.

Joshua stood tall among the others.

"He doesn't look any worse for the wear," Miriam commented.

Eliora relaxed by her side.

"We have returned from spying out the land," Joshua reported in his deep voice.

The crowd cheered though none louder than Eliora in Miriam's ear.

She gave her friend a sideways glance.

"Sorry," the midwife whispered.

"Since it is the time of the first grapes, we have brought back fruit from the land." Joshua waved his men forward.

"Oh my," Eliora whispered. "Would you look at that."

Miriam didn't believe her eyes. She blinked a few times, rubbed them, and blinked a few more times.

Two men carried a staff between their shoulders. On the staff hung a cluster of grapes so large it nearly scraped the ground.

"These are from the brook of Eshcol plucked by my own two hands." Joshua held up his hands to accent his point. "We went into the land you sent us. It surely does flow with milk and honey as the Lord has said and this is the fruit of it." He waved to another man.

The other stepped forward with a large sack of figs and pomegranates which he held open for all to see.

"Look at the size of those," Eliora commented. "They are bigger than my fist."

"Bigger than your head," Miriam teased.

People stepped closer to see the fruit for themselves.

"However, it is not all good news," Joshua continued. "The people who dwell in the land are strong. The cities are walled and very great. We also saw the children of Anak there."

The people backed up.

Miriam searched the crowd. She found fear and confusion on many of their faces.

"The Amalekites dwell in the south lands," Joshua went on. "The Hittites, Jebusites, and the Amorites all dwell in the mountains as well."

Murmurings grew louder.

Caleb raised his hands and motioned for the people to be silent. "Let us go up now and possess this land for we are able to have the victory."

"We can't have the victory," Shammua argued. "The people are much stronger than us."

"They are men of great stature," Palti added as he stretched up on his toes and lifted his hand high above his head to make his point.

"They were giants, sons of Anak," Sethur confirmed. "We were like grasshoppers in their sight."

Joshua's attention flew to each man as he spoke. He looked to Caleb, who shook in head violently.

"Please," Moses attempted to calm the men. "Let us discuss this."

"There nothing to discuss," Shammua replied. "We have seen it with our own eyes. You have not."

"If you send us to fight," Igal said. "We will all

surely perish."

"God should have let us die in the land of Egypt," a man from the crowd called out.

"Or in the wilderness," a woman added.

"Why has the Lord brought us to this land to die by the sword?" another man cried. "That our wives and children should be prey. It would have been better for us to return to Egypt."

Agreements shouted from every corner of the crowd.

"Let's choose another leader and go back to Egypt," Gaddi offered.

Moses and Aaron fell on their face in the dust.

Joshua and Caleb rent their outer garments.

"The land which we searched is an exceedingly good land," Joshua reasoned. "If the Lord delights in us then He will bring us into the land He promised us."

"Don't rebel against the Lord," Caleb added. "And don't fear the people of the land. They are bread for us. Their defense is departed from them. The Lord is with us." He beat his chest with his fist. "Don't be afraid of them."

The people crowded closer toward them. Many of them picked up stones as they advanced.

Eliora tightened her grip on Miriam's arm.

Miriam took a step in front of her friend and pushed her behind herself.

The cloud moved to cover Moses, Aaron,

Joshua, and Caleb.

"How long will these people provoke Me?" the cloud boomed toward Moses. "How long will it be before they believe Me? Have I not provided enough signs and wonders for their proof?" Thunder and sparks flew from the cloud pressing back the crowd. "I will smite them with a pestilence. I will disinherit them. I will make you a greater nation and mightier than all of them combined."

"Forbid it, Lord," Moses pleaded. "If you do those things then the Egyptians will hear and will tell it to the inhabitants of this land. They have all heard how great You are among our people. How You speak with us face to face and how Your presence in the pillar of cloud and fire has never left us and leads us night and day."

He raised a hand to his face to block the bright lightning flashes. "If You kill these people and leave only me left, the nations will hear of it and say You weren't strong enough to bring the people into the land You promised to them."

His voice rose in timbre, "I beg You, according to Your great mercy, that You forgive these people and their iniquity."

Everyone held their breath for the silence of several heartbeats.

"I have pardoned according to your pleas," the voice boomed. "But as truly as I live, all the earth will be filled with My glory. These men, to whom I've shown all the miracles, have tempted me ten times and have not obeyed My voice. Assuredly, they will not see the land which I promised to their fathers. Neither any of them that provoked Me will see the land. Only Caleb and Joshua will see the land because they have followed me fully."

Moses wept.

"Tomorrow you will turn yourself away," the voice continued. "How long shall I bear this evil congregation who murmurs against me? I have heard your request to not enter the land. I will do what you have requested. Your carcasses will fall in this wilderness and all of you twenty years old and upward will not come into the land."

Aaron whimpered.

"Your children will I bring into the land which you have despised. Your children will wander in the wilderness for forty years, bearing your transgressions until every one of your bodies fall in the sands. For every day you searched the land, even forty, that will be the number of years they will bear your iniquities."

Thunders roared and flashes struck out from the cloud.

The ten men standing with Joshua and Caleb fell ill from the sight. Others returned to their tents.

Miriam sat with her brothers in Moses' tent for

the rest of the day.

The silence was heavy as none of them knew what to say to ease the burden they all felt.

As darkness fell outside, Joshua entered the tent with a bow.

Moses rose to meet him.

"All of the ten other spies have died," his solemn tone and hefty words added to the weight in the room.

Moses knelt were he stood.

Joshua placed a hand on his shoulder.

Miriam could see her brother's shoulders heave up and down.

The young warrior turned and left.

Miriam crawled to her brother's side and lifted one of his arms over her shoulder. She let him weep until he quieted.

"What was it all for?" she asked just above a whisper. She waited until he met her gaze. "To die out here?" Tears blurred her vision.

"Sometimes with God, the answer is wait."

She hugged him tight and then left for her own tent.

When she entered her personal space, she sat down and wrapped her arms around her knees. She rocked herself as she remembered everything the voice in the cloud pillar had declared.

"Miriam?" Eliora called a few moments later.

"Yes."

The young woman entered solemnly. "I wasn't sure if you wanted company."

She thought for a moment, then patted the ground next to her.

Eliora sat and folded her hands in her lap. She stared at her part of the rug they had sewn earlier. She reached over and brushed it lightly.

Miriam saw her fingers tremble. She pulled her friend in close and held on to her.

"Their moment of disobedience will cost us all a lifetime to pay for it," Eliora whimpered into Miriam's hair.

She rocked her friend. "Don't say such things."

"You heard Moses," she defended. "Of course, you must have heard it straight from the cloud's mouth. 'Anyone over twenty is going to die out here.' That includes me." She wept.

"Shh," Miriam comforted.

"At least your sin only cost you a week."

She held on tight. Her heart ached. There were no words to comfort her friend because she had no words to comfort herself. The Lord been clear Anyone over twenty except Joshua and Caleb would fall in the wilderness. They would not see the promised land.

She let the tears flow freely. Her heart raced as she wept. Her mouth hung open as she wailed for what she would miss. All the trials she had lived through in Egypt and all the hardness in the wilderness had led them here. Just one river crossing away from the promised land.

Chapter 22

"And they said one to another, 'Let us make a captain, and let us return into Egypt.' "
-NUMBERS 14:4

Miriam rose early to collect her portion of manna for the day. Her shoulders fell heavy with the unseen burden. Her fingers moved slowly as she picked up the pieces of heaven frost. She had hoped the time to gather would be done and she would soon be planting her own garden. Her fingers ached to dig deep into rich soil again. She brushed sand from her hands.

Her attention caught a group forming near the end of the camp. She rose and went to them when she saw Moses approach the men.

"Are you going to sin further?" Moses pleaded with them. "Don't go that way. Your plan will not prosper because the Lord is not with you. You will fall before your enemies because you have turned away from the Lord."

"We are heading back to Egypt," Jareb replied.

He lifted his pack to his back. "What difference does it make whether we die trying or die in the wilderness?"

He turned and led the group toward a distant mountain.

"What are they doing?" Miriam stood by her brother.

"They are heading up into the mountains to go back," he explained and then turned to face her. "The Lord warned me that their plan will fail."

"You've got to stop them." She stepped to follow the group.

"I tried." He sighed. "They've made their choice."

"So that's it?"

He nodded and faced toward the camp.

"We just let them die?" she whispered to his back.

He kept walking.

Miriam prayed for the Lord to turn the group's steps back toward the safety of the camp. She watched as long as their forms could be seen. When she couldn't see them anymore, she returned to her tent.

"All of them?" Miriam covered her mouth.

Eliora had brought word about the group of people who left camp the day before.

"That was the report." Tears poured over the edges of her eyes. "The group died at the hands of the Amalekites and the Canaanites who dwell on the hill."

Miriam mourned for their families. She made a mental list of those she would visit the following day. It would only be the beginning of those who would fall in the wilderness. Her heart ached at the thought and grief deepened its grasp.

"Do you really think He meant everyone?" Eliora's question brought Miriam's thought back to the conversation.

"I think the Lord always means what He says."

"There's no going back."

Miriam knew it wasn't a question.

"There's no going forward." The midwife met her eyes. "There is just this wilderness."

She nodded. Her friend suddenly looked years older than she really was.

They sat still for several heartbeats each pondering the sorrow of their sentence.

A stirring outside brought their attention to the tent flap.

"What's that?" Eliora edged closer to her friend.

Miriam shrugged. "It's the Sabbath. Everyone should be resting."

"That doesn't sound like resting."

Miriam rose with Eliora right behind her. She peeled back the flap to look around.

A group of men was dragging another toward the gate of the tabernacle.

Moses and Aaron came out of Moses' tent at the sound of the commotion.

"What is the meaning of this?" Moses asked.

Miriam and Eliora came to stand near Aaron.

"This man was found gathering sticks on the Sabbath," Lyron declared.

Moses looked at the man. "Is this true?"

He kept his head down, but the bundle of sticks under his arm was proof enough.

"Did you know that this was forbidden?"

Priel nodded slowly.

Moses stepped into the courtyard before the cloud that was above the inner tent.

Miriam watched as he prayed and then fell silent for several minutes.

When he turned back, she saw his fallen countenance and fear gripped her.

"The Lord has spoken." He stepped to Priel. "This man shall be stoned to death."

"No, please." He fell to his knees and pulled on the hem of Moses' outer coat.

"Take him."

The group dragged the man off screaming.

Miriam stepped to her brother. "Why?"

He lifted his head and she saw tears filling his eyes. "It's not my choice."

"But stoning?"

"It's what the Lord has said." He shut his lids and held them tight. "He's angry with us. We have all sinned so greatly. He's given so many warnings…"

Miriam listened to the screams in the distance until they were silenced by the sound of rocks smashing into each other. Then everything was still once again.

She returned her gaze to her brother.

"Go back to your tent and obey the Sabbath," he whispered. "Please."

She nodded.

He walked away slowly.

She could almost feel the burden that hung on his shoulders. It felt as if the same weight were on her own.

The following morning, Moses came to Miriam and called her from her tent.

"I need you to gather the women."

She tilted her head at him.

"The Lord has instructed for us to make blue fringes on the borders of our garments."

"Why?"

"So we can remember all the commandments of the Lord and obey them. So we remember Him and all He has done for us. So that we don't have a repeat like yesterday…" His words trailed off.

She reached for his arm. "I'll see to it."

"Thank you." He placed a rough hand on hers.

Miriam sent word for Eliora to bring her clothes and meet her.

The midwife entered Miriam's tent with her arms full of dresses. "Blue tassels?" She set them down and inspected the border of one.

"That's what he said." Miriam gathered her own collection of dresses.

"All of them?" Eliora looked over the stack.

She nodded. "Let's get over to Orpah's tent."

"I thought we were working here."

"I've called for them to meet us there," Miriam explained. "Orpah is the best seam worker I know."

"She does do fine work."

"I figured she would help us with some of the more difficult garments."

Eliora picked up her pile of clothes and followed Miriam down the path. "And this is supposed to help us remember?"

"I guess since we wear clothes every day that when we see the blue, then we will remember the commandments."

"If you say so."

They reached the woman's large tent.

"It is good to see you." Orpah welcomed them each with a kiss on the cheek.

"Thank you for helping us," Miriam said.

"My pleasure." She waved them into the tent. "Always happy to help."

Other women joined, each with armfuls or sacks of clothes to work.

Miriam sat next to Eliora. They watched Orpah twist tassels with expert hands and then skillfully attach them to a garment.

After the quick lesson, everyone set to work on their own piles.

Miriam ran her fingers over an old dress. "Hmm."

"What?"

"I've never patched this dress," she said, but kept turning the dress over in her hands.

Eliora examined the dress she was adding a tassel to. "I haven't patched this one either."

Miriam looked around at all the women sitting with piles of clothing.

"Has anyone had to patch any of the clothes they brought with them?" she asked.

Each woman filtered through their piles for a few moments. Then they returned silent glances to Miriam.

"No one?" She raised an eyebrow.

Heads shook around the circle.

"It's been two years and no one has to patch a single garment?"

Realization settled around the tent.

"God has been providing for us in so many ways that we didn't even realize," she remarked.

Eliora stood and held one of the garments with new tassels against the front of her body. She rocked side to side to make the tassels sway. "I don't think the blue matches this dress."

"I don't think that's the point," Miriam reminded her with a chuckle.

Chapter 23

"And all the children of Israel murmured against Moses and against Aaron…"
-NUMBERS 14:2

"You and Aaron have taken too much authority upon yourself," Korah accused as he stood outside Moses' tent.

The loud voices had drawn Miriam from hers.

"We all are just as holy as you," he continued without waiting for Moses to defend himself. "The Lord is among us. Yet, you raise yourself above us all."

Miriam recognized many of the faces among the large group. Brothers Dathan and Abiram and their cousin, On, were of the tribe of Reuben though Korah was her own kin.

"Tomorrow." Moses knelt before them. "The Lord will show you who belongs to Himself and who is holy."

The group left with bitterness still dripping from their lingering words.

Miriam reached for her brother's elbow to help him rise. "What are you doing?"

"The Lord will fight for me just as He did for us at the Red Sea."

"What did they want?"

He brushed some sand from his tunic. "Power."

The following morning, Miriam gathered with others by the gate of the tabernacle.

Eliora's gaze landed to Joshua, who stood beside Moses before she let her glance fall to the ground.

Miriam opened her mouth to ask the cause of her friend's downturned expression but decided to save her question for a more private moment. Instead, she turned her attention on Korah.

"Cousin, why are you doing this?" she pleaded.

Korah simply stared at her sideways.

"Please don't do this."

"Hold your peace, sister," Aaron said in her ear. "Let the Lord handle them."

"Each of you take a censer and put fire in them," Moses ordered. "Whomever the Lord chooses that person will be holy." He looked over at his cousin. "Hear me, Korah, it seems a small thing to you that the God of Israel has separated you from the rest of the congregation for service in the tabernacle. Yet you come near to demand priesthood as well?"

Korah straightened his shoulders making himself appear taller.

"What is Aaron that you murmur against him?" Moses waved to his brother.

Aaron stood in silence.

"And where are Dathan and Abiram that gathered with you yesterday?" He searched among the group of men. "Send for them."

Two men left and returned minutes later.

"They refuse to come," one reported.

Moses shook his head. "Even they choose not to stand with such foolishness."

Korah folded his arms across his broad chest.

Moses turned toward the cloud pillar and prayed, "Lord, do not respect their offering. I have not taken anything from them nor hurt any of them." He listened to the thunderings for a few moments before he turned to face Aaron. "He wants us to separate ourselves from the congregation so He can judge them."

Aaron shook.

"Oh God, the God of the spirits of all flesh," Moses prayed. "Because of one man's sin will You be angry with the entire congregation?"

Moses walked past Miriam, leaving through the gate.

"Where are you going?" She reached out for him.

"To the tent of Dathan and Abiram," he stated

clearly.

Miriam followed.

"Depart," Moses called into the tents as he neared the ones that belonged to Dathan and Abiram. "God has called all to depart from the tents of these wicked men and touch nothing of theirs unless you wish to be consumed in all their sins."

People scattered in all directions like a spooked herd.

Miriam took a few steps back but stood near enough to keep her brother within her sight.

Dathan and Abiram came out of their tent and stood before Moses with their wives and children.

"By this, you will know that the Lord has sent me for none of this has been my idea," he spoke with authority. "If these men die by natural means, then the Lord has not sent me. But if the Lord does an unknown thing and the earth opens her mouth to swallow them." He pointed to the group. "Then you will understand that these men have provoked the Lord."

The ground under Miriam's feet shook. She looked to the group standing in front of Moses. They were looking to the ground under their feet too. As it split, Moses stepped backward.

Miriam grasped his arm and pulled him away.

Screams came as the group of people standing with Dathan and Abiram fell into the pit. Even the tents fell into the opening.

Just as quickly as the land had opened, it closed up again like a mouth opening and closing over a morsel of food.

Sounds of crackling made them turn back to the tabernacle. Fire sparked from the cloud pillar.

Moses looked at Miriam. The two started running back at the same time.

When they arrived, Moses stopped Miriam before she could get close. But it was too late. In front of the gate of the tabernacle lay the charred remains of the two hundred and fifty men that stood with Korah. His body too, lay burned among the others.

Miriam covered her mouth but not before a scream escaped.

Moses held onto her as she pressed against him.

"No!"

"Go no further, sister," Moses ordered.

She wailed.

"Eleazer!"

The man appeared beside them.

"Take the censers out of the pile. Scatter the fire so that it burns whatever is left." He allowed himself a glance at the scene and then returned to his instructions. "Take the censers and make them into a broad plate as a covering for the altar. It will serve as a reminder that only the seed of Aaron can come near to offer incense before the Lord."

Eleazer nodded and set to his task.

Moses turned his gaze to Miriam.

Her eyes burned with tears and she still held her hands over her mouth. "Our family."

"They came against the Lord," he answered her unspoken question. "He has to judge."

"There are none of them left."

He closed his eyes and shook his head. "I know."

"Are there going to be any of us left?"

Moses pulled her in close.

She leaned on his chest and wept.

Voices roused Miriam with the early rays of the sun. Her heart sank. She rose and found another group of men gathered with Moses.

"You have killed the people of the Lord," a man accused as he stuck his finger in Moses' face.

Moses and Aaron looked toward the cloud pillar.

Miriam found her gaze turning there as well.

Thunders roared. Lightning flashed.

Moses and Aaron looked at each other.

"Take a censer with fire from the altar and put incense in it quickly," Moses instructed his brother. "Bring it among the congregation to make atonement for them. God's wrath is sending out a plague even as we speak."

Flashes came from the cloud as people fell ill all around them.

Miriam reached out for a woman who had fainted beside her.

A man collapsed dead at her feet.

She met Moses' fearful eyes.

Aaron hurried into the gate and returned with a censer that smoked with incense.

Even more people fell all around.

Aaron rushed into the middle of the group.

"Right there," Moses said, holding up his hand.

People on the other side stood waiting to see if they would also fall.

Aaron stood still, holding out the censer. His chest rose and fell in quick heaves. He was frozen in place awaiting further commands.

"The plague has stopped," Moses finally said.

Aaron relaxed his arm and returned to the tabernacle.

"Help us round these people up," he called to a group standing nearby.

The men carried bodies out of the camp for hours.

Miriam stood leaning upon one of the posts of the tabernacle.

"How many?" Moses asked the tired man covered with sweat as he approached in the dying light of the day.

"Fourteen thousand and seven hundred." The man wiped his brow with the back of his hand.

Moses nodded and waved him off.

He turned to see Miriam.

She met his gaze for a moment before closing her eyes.

When she opened them again, her brother still stood staring at her.

She shook her head and went back to her tent.

When will it end, Lord?

Chapter 24

*"And it shall come to pass, that the man's rod,
whom I shall choose, shall blossom…"*
-NUMBERS 17:5

A scream stirred Miriam from her tent. Aaron's form swayed in the moonlight. She ran to him.

"What is it, brother?"

His eyes were large and wild. "A dream."

She nodded. Far too many of her own dreams had roused her from slumber.

She reached out to steady him. "Tell me about it."

He blinked a few times staring into her face.

"I stood before a sea of faces as they murmured for change." He shook his head. "Moses had been in the cloud for weeks with no sign of return. The people begged me to do something—anything."

The skin on Miriam's arms tingled. She knew his dream was a haunting reminder of his long-ago sin.

"I told them to fetch gold from among them

and bring it to me. The flood of faces ebbed and flowed like a wave upon the shore bringing with it several golden objects which washed up to my feet."

Miriam's thoughts painted the picture quite clearly.

"After I collected the pieces, I threw them into a burning fire. The solid forms melted to the point they could be molded. Skillfully, I shaped the gold in my hands until it formed a calf." He moved his hands around mimicking the movements.

"As I finished, I stepped back to inspect the work." His large eyes held hers. "That's when I noticed smudges all over the small cow. I picked up a nearby rag to brighten the gold. I started to polish the metal, but noticed that the fingerprints and smudges would not disappear. In fact, the more I polished, the more I saw my prints deepen into the gold." His breath turned into a pant.

She rubbed his back.

"I worked until perspiration poured from my brow, but the golden calf was covered in the deep grooves of my own fingerprints. Defeated, I stepped back to stare into the lifeless face of the calf. The eyes of the animal glowed as if they were red-hot flames. The mouth opened wide and sought to swallow me." He grabbed his tunic and pulled it away from his chest.

She held him tight.

"That's when I woke up…screaming."

Miriam rubbed his untamed hair down to comfort the trembling man in her arms.

"This isn't the first time I've had this dream," he spoke when his quivers ceased.

She waited for him to continue.

"Almost every night since it happened, but not like tonight."

Her own heart raced at the many visions the Lord had given her in her dreams. They could be so real. "Do you think it's because of the test tomorrow?"

He nodded. "I was heading to talk to Moses."

"I think that's a good idea."

Moses stepped out of his tent at their call. "The dream again?"

Aaron nodded, but kept his head bowed toward the sand.

"You've been forgiven," he reassured him.

Miriam gave his hand a supportive squeeze.

Aaron dared a peek toward the direction of the Tabernacle. "What do you think will happen in the morning?"

His eyes fell on the pillar of fire burning bright. He followed it up to the dark speckled sky and then back to the covered tent.

"I'm not sure." He sighed. "I'm honestly not sure."

Aaron closed his eyes.

Miriam guessed at what he might be thinking.

With the accusation hurled against Aaron's right to be priest, the people had demanded a test. God had given instructions for each person's name to be carved into their rods and placed in the inner tent. She remembered Aaron's rod which bore his name and imagined it lying among the eleven others. *What would morning's light reveal? Would this sign finally be enough to appease the people's restlessness?*

"Our God is a consuming fire," Moses interrupted her thoughts.

Aaron finally looked into the face of his younger brother.

"When He touches something," he continued. "It must change. As the tongues of a fire lick at the offerings or a wildfire spreads through the land, things change, are burned, melted, or completely destroyed. Regardless, it's always different."

Aaron's gaze went back to the Tabernacle.

Miriam looked to the blazing pillar that shone bright as their nightly safeguard.

"Go rest." Moses patted his brother's shoulder.

He nodded.

Miriam met his glance. She wanted to say more in order to provide greater comfort to her brother, but nothing further was needed. God would be the one to provide the sign. There was nothing she could do to change the outcome.

The next morning, Miriam stood beside her nervous brother.

Aaron wrung his hands and stroked his beard.

She stretched out a hand and squeezed his arm.

He patted hers with his free hand, but didn't turn to her.

Moses arrived and together the two men walked into the tent.

Miriam held her breath as she waited for her brothers to come back out.

When their forms appeared again, she stretched her neck to inspect the rods in their hands. The bundle that Moses carried were empty and as plain as when they had entered. He handed each of the eleven rods to the man whose name it bore.

Aaron stood still with his eyes on his rod.

Miriam noticed Aaron's rod was covered in stunning white blossoms. Several of the buds had also produced large, brown almonds. The honey-sweet fragrance filled the gentle breeze. She inhaled it deeply and longed to pick one of the nuts to taste for herself.

"The Lord's fingerprints are more fruitful than ours could ever hope to be," Moses encouraged.

She smiled at her brothers.

"My fingerprints brought nothing but sin and destruction," Aaron replied as he stroked the velvety soft blossoms. "The Lord's fingerprints have taken a dead stick and, not only produced life, but produced a harvest."

Moses nodded. "Now that we have that matter settled." He turned toward the group of priests. "Let us move forward with the sacrifice."

Miriam watched a large man lead the calf forward through the gate of the tabernacle. The proud owner stood tall next to the docile animal.

The red heifer was perfect. Its coat was clean and her dark eyes were bright and clear. The young animal had never experienced a hard day's work. She had been born and bred for this day. Nothing was required of her except to keep the blood pumping through her heart at least for a few more minutes.

The man handed the loose rope to Eleazar.

Miriam's nephew inspected the animal over with a careful eye and then gave a sharp nod to his father and uncle Moses.

"Take her outside the camp," Moses' voice was firm. "Bring back the blood."

The man followed Eleazer and the animal

away from the tabernacle.

Everyone who stood witness waited patiently.

Miriam heard the quick bellow of the animal for one brief moment. With such practice, the priests had become efficient in their duty.

Eleazar returned with a large vessel full of blood. He dipped his finger in and sprinkled the blood before the tabernacle seven times.

The priests who had added cedarwood, hyssop, and scarlet cords onto the fire which burned the remains outside the camp, together with the man who had offered the heifer, all went to their tents to purify themselves as Moses had instructed.

Miriam followed her brother to the place outside the camp where the fire was dying down.

Burning cedarwood carried on the wind to Miriam's nose, but the sweet scent was quickly overtaken by the not so pleasant odors from the animal's hide that mixed with it.

A priest collected the ashes and gave them to Moses.

"This is to be the waters of separation," Moses taught. "If someone touches a dead body, they will be unclean seven days. Then they can sprinkle some of the red heifer ash mixed with clean water on themselves. With a hyssop branch, they need to sprinkle the tent of the dead person and any uncovered vessels. Once they have done this, they need to wash themselves and their clothes and they shall be clean once more and not be cut off from Israel."

Miriam shook her head. Another process to follow. Another set of guidelines handed down to remind them just how unclean they truly were in the eyes of a holy God.

The reminder of the weight of sin on her generation was too much. She stepped away toward her tent.

"Miriam," a familiar voice called after her.

She turned to meet Eliora's face.

"Your brother sure comes up with some strange methods." She quickly caught up with her pace.

"God," Miriam corrected.

Eliora hesitated a step. "Sometimes I wonder."

She gave her friend a sideways glance.

"Not that I would ever-"

"Eliora!" a shrill scream came from somewhere among the tents.

The midwife glanced around quickly trying to find the path that would take her toward the call.

"Eliora!" the voice screamed again.

"That way." Miriam pointed.

They came upon a woman searching tents.

"Maven!" Eliora yelled to the frantic woman.

"Thank the Lord." She clasped her hands together and ran toward them.

"What is it?" Eliora asked.

"It's Riva. She is starting her pains."

"Riva?" Miriam asked.

The young woman nodded.

"You know her?" Eliora inquired.

"She's my sister-in-law. My brother, Aaron, is married to her husband's sister, Elisheba."

"Hurry," Maven urged.

"Care to come along then?" Eliora offered. "Since she's family."

Miriam nodded and the three of them rushed together toward the tents of Judah.

Eliora beat the other two inside the tent.

Miriam entered behind her. She saw Riva bent over holding her midsection.

The midwife was already by her side helping her straighten out.

"Miriam," the pregnant woman panted. "It's good to see you."

"You as well." She pointed to the woman's stomach. "Close?"

She nodded then a pain shook her.

"Let me see just how close." Eliora positioned the woman to check her progress.

A few hours later, Riva delivered a healthy baby.

Eliora cleaned the boy with oil and water and wrapped him in a fresh linen.

"A son," Riva whispered a sigh of

contentment. "Nahshon will be so pleased."

"Would you like to meet your new nephew?" Eliora held the bundle out to Miriam.

Miriam looked to Riva.

She nodded. A smile widened across her face.

Miriam molded her arms to cradle the newborn.

Eliora lifted the baby into her arms. "Mind his head."

Miriam adjusted her arm to give extra support. She looked into the deep, dark almond-shaped eyes of the boy in her arms. "He's so beautiful," she whispered.

When she was sure she could bear his weight in her one arm, she lifted the other carefully and traced the bridge of his nose with her finger.

The boy cooed at her touch.

She smiled at him and he seemed to mimic her facial movements. The expression made her giggle.

He made a sound that danced in her ears. It was a content and happy noise.

Tears filled her eyes and she looked up to Eliora. "Is this what it's like to bring life into the world?"

Eliora nodded. "When it goes as smooth as this, yes."

"What's his name?" she asked Riva.

"Salmon."

"I like it," Eliora remarked.

Miriam looked back to the young one in her arms. "Me too."

His pink lips turned into a circle with a large yawn.

She nuzzled his face and hummed in his ear the song she had sung after they crossed the Red Sea as she slowly danced around the small space.

"You, my dear Salmon," she said upon finishing her song. "Will get to walk the land of promise."

Epilogue

"… and the people abode in Kadesh…"
-NUMBERS 20:1

1406 B.C.

Thirteen thousand five hundred and ninety times, Miriam watched the sun set on the wilderness of Paran. For forty years, she woke every morning waiting for news of who would need to be buried that day. She watched men and women fall in the sands of the desert. Everyone. Just as God had said.

She stood at the edge of the camp, where she watched a meeting between Joshua, Caleb, and Salmon. The two older men were teaching the younger. Their conversation was deep and not meant for her ears.

The sun caught a glint in Salmon's young eyes. He was intently listening to the instruction of the other two as an apprentice learning his trade.

Miriam noted the dark beard that framed his

broad chin. His hair had taken on a curl with its length.

The two other men stood in stark contrast to the youth. Their beards and hair were washed white with age. Their once smooth skin was now wrinkled by time. They each looked as though they could be Salmon's grandfather.

Salmon's tanned olive skin was smooth and robust. Though, by Moses' suggestion, he had taken his place among the warrior leaders, he had seen no fighting. According to Moses, that would change very soon.

Her heart skipped a beat thinking of the baby she held in her arms only moments after his birth heading into battle. But he was no longer a baby and he did not belong to her. She had not bore him. Joshua and Caleb would teach him well and he would need every moment of their instruction.

Looking over Joshua's broad frame. Her heart ached picturing young Eliora next to him. She had died in the wilderness just as she feared. Joshua had never come to take her as a wife. Also, as she feared.

Miriam smiled at the image that never was. Eliora old and long retired from assisting births standing tall and proud next to her humble warrior. Maybe with a few children and even grandchildren of their own running around. She shook the image away.

Only the three men stood in a half-circle discussing strategy remained. Joshua had never married and there were no such plans in his agenda as far as Miriam had known. He was dedicated to the Lord and he took it as seriously as breathing.

Caleb had taken a lovely wife who had produced him heirs to expand the tents of the tribe of Judah. She too didn't make it through the wilderness, but his children were counted among those who would settle in Canaan.

Emptiness picked at the edges in Miriam's heart. No man had ever asked her to join him on the journey of life. Possibly either too terrified of her leadership team of brothers or some lack of her own of which she was unaware. In any event, she stood on her own walking the way where God led.

She wondered again at Salmon. He was handsome, though she probably thought she was much too partial. He had been the only baby she held outside of her two brothers. She wondered what kind of woman would stand by his side. She had seen so many girls grow into fine women, but none had caught his eye. She wondered if he was following in Joshua's footsteps in more ways than one.

She sighed and set her steps toward her tent.

So many new faces crowded the paths between

the tents as she walked. No one was over the age of forty besides the two older men she had just left to their meeting, her two brothers who would be finishing their work in the tabernacle as the sun inched its last few steps toward the horizon, and herself.

They had settled in the same place they had come forty years earlier just on the other side of Jordan from Canaan. The goal upon leaving Egypt so long ago was in sight.

In the one hundred and twenty-seven years of her life, Miriam had endured plagues in Egypt, thirst and hunger in the wilderness, plagues on her people, leprosy of her own skin, and many things in between. The most condemning judgment of all was the routine of forty years of simply waiting for all those sentenced to die.

No more miraculous signs. No more fresh words from God. Oh, the pillar of cloud and fire still led them whenever and wherever it chose. Manna still covered the ground to feed them every morning. Water was still found to quench their thirst. Clothes still kept their shape and strength. Even their bodies did not ache with their many, many steps, but nothing new. Simply day after day of burials.

Only the five of them remained from their generation. God had promised only two of them would walk the dusty roads of the promised land.

Though Miriam secretly wished somehow God had overlooked her and her two siblings in His count. The other part of her wondered which sibling would bury the others.

Standing in the place of those fallen were sons and daughters. It was almost time to enter the land promised to their ancestor Abraham so many years ago. The next morning would find them marching toward Canaan.

Entering her simple tent, she laid her head down on her mat. She breathed in the cool, crisp air of the desert.

In all her years, she never thought she'd ever see the promise to Abraham fulfilled. She thought she'd always live in Egypt, allowing some other generation to taste freedom. That day had come and gone more than forty years ago. She never thought she'd be this close to it now. Their people's land lay just on the other side of the Jordan River. It had been waiting for its true occupants to claim it back from the pagan people who used it for their own fleshly pleasure.

A land flowing with milk and honey. Her mouth watered at the reminder of feasting on those grapes she had seen carried by Joshua and Caleb. They were larger than her fist. She smiled, wondering what other delicious treasures awaited her.

No more manna. She almost laughed aloud at

the delight that the thought brought.

Her heart ached with such longing she couldn't bear it. Sleep did not come easy. She wanted to stay up all night thinking of the wonders that lay ahead of her. But she'd need her sleep for the journey.

She closed her eyes and imagined what it would be like to step foot on the fertile soil of Canaan. To feel the rich moisture squish between her toes. To inhale so deeply the fragrance of wildflowers and crops.

Moses was right. She thought to herself as she slowed her breathing. *With God, sometimes the answer is wait.*

A Note to You

Dear Reader,

Sadly, Miriam didn't make it to the promised land. She died at the "11th hour" before heading into Canaan. God promised only Joshua and Caleb would lead the second generation to walk that sought out land. This included not only the rebellious first generation, but the three siblings who led them.

Aaron and Moses would soon follow their sister in death on this side of the Jordan. None of them tasted Canaan for themselves, but they had another promised land waiting for them.

The consequences of sin are often deadly because God designed them that way to deter us from their grip. We all find ourselves caught in sin's trap from time to time, but we must remember that God has promised to provide a way out of every temptation according to 1 Corinthians 10:13.

With God, sometimes the answer is wait, but sometimes the answer is no. Miriam didn't get to walk into Canaan as one of its new residents, but she stepped into glory to meet the God she had followed for over one hundred and twenty years. She finally got to see Him face to face.

~Jenifer Jennings

Want to find out what happens next?

Rahab's god didn't come to her rescue. An enemy's God is asking for her trust.

When her family's plan for her future dissolves, Rahab is forced on a dark path. Working as a harlot provides her a comfortable, though empty life.

As the Israelite army marches toward Jericho, Rahab must choose between the city she loves and an unknown God chasing after her.

Stand with Rahab in Book 3 of the Faith Finders Series, *Crimson Cord* as she waits to see if her faith will hold while her crimson cord blows in the wind.

Also by Jenifer Jennings

* * *

Faith Finders Series:
Go deeper into the stories of these familiar faith heroines.

Midwives of Moses
Wilderness Wanderer
Crimson Cord
A Stolen Wife
At His Feet
Lasting Legacy

* * *

Servant Siblings Series:
They were Jesus' siblings,
but they become His followers.

James
Joseph
Assia
Jude
Lydia
Simon
Salome

* * *

Thank You!

Hubby, thank you for your sacrificial love for me, for our family, and for our hopes and dreams. Without you, I could do none of this. I love you.

Kids, thank you for showing me the reason why I fight for my dreams. As I see you grow, I want you to see me as an example of hard work and striving for what God has laid on the heart.

Word Weavers Clay County, you gals never cease to amaze me with your suggestions. Thank you for the prayers and critiques over this project.

Betas: Rob and Katherine, thank you for your opinions when this story was fresh and new. Your honest critiques helped polish this work.

Jenifer's Jewels (ARC Team), your positivity is a constant source of encouragement to me. Thank you.

About the Author

Jenifer Jennings is a passionate storyteller who brings ancient worlds to life through Biblical historical novels. A devoted student of Scripture since coming to faith in Jesus at seventeen, she holds a bachelor's degree in Women's Ministry and a master's in Biblical Languages. Jenifer is an active member of Word Weavers International, serving as an online chapter president, and a member of American Christian Fiction Writers (ACFW). When Jenifer's not writing, she's on a date with her husband or mothering their two children, a wise-cracking mathematician and a feisty artist.

If you'd like to keep up with new releases, receive spiritual encouragement, and get your hands on a FREE book, then join Jenifer's Newsletter at:
jeniferjennings.com/gift

www.ingramcontent.com/pod-product-compliance
Lightning Source LLC
Chambersburg PA
CBHW060541180626
46817CB00002B/666